Angelina's Bottom

Kristian Himmelstrup

Translated from the Danish by
Nina Sokol

Spuyten Duyvil

New York City

Special thanks to The Danish Arts Foundation for financial support towards the translation and publication of this book.

The story we have for you here is really divided into two parts. The first part could be omitted, but it gives us some preliminary information which is useful.
From "Heartache" by Hans Christian Andersen (translated by Jean Hirsholt)

They can all go to hell and I'll go to Texas.
David Crockett

Arrival

He arrives in Houston late in the evening. He is tired. He hasn't slept for almost two days now and it feels as though he is living in a glass bubble of jet lag and clogged-up ears.

He walks out onto the swaying jet bridge that has just been connected to the airplane like a mechanical caterpillar. It sways as if it were a bad omen. A warm breeze from the tropical, humid air of the early evening seeps through the cracks and he takes a deep breath. Through the small windows he can discern the setting sun. It is almost five o'clock. In front of him is a small, obese family talking in loud voices with their Southern drawl. The father is wearing a cowboy hat and the youngest son a t-shirt with the picture of a Winchester rifle on it and a couple of cartridges on his back.

He sighs. He still hasn't fully left Denmark. He is standing with one foot on the escalator in Kastrupas, his sister and wife stand a few meters away from him, waving, tears rolling down their cheeks. The last steps up the escalator are the hardest. It is as though that single step is the decisive factor determining that he is to be away for two years and that the escalator carries the blame for ensuring that the punishment is executed. He feels he no longer has a say in the matter and suddenly doesn't know how he ended up here in front of the escalator cranking their endless steps ready to transport him directly into the unknown.

"What if we don't like each other anymore when I return?" he whispers.

"What if we have grown apart? Changed?" she answers, as though that were the only unfortunate thing that might happen. Which it is for the person he is now who must once again be sacrificed for the cause of his life with a new developmental adjustment. It's not the first time he's been there and he has come to fear the coming farewell already on the way out, at the foot of the escalating stairs, the coffee at Karen Blixen Bar, the meandering queue at the check-in where they have already said everything they wanted to say. Three times.

He looks up. He has entered a big tunnel with blue carpeting and white walls. A yellow stripe on the floor directs him to the right but the people in front of him have stopped moving. The obese family is already standing still, the boys with their heavy arms hanging limply by their sides and their tired gazes resting on the carpet. He positions himself behind them, as the last person in line. It occurs to him that he is always the last person in line. Every so often they lean to the side to see what's going on in front of the line but it's impossible to see where it ends. Thirty meters further up it turns at a corner which he assumes must be close to the exit. Welcome to the United States of America, it says with worn letters. A German in a pin-striped suit leans against the wall but is shooed away by a heavy, black woman in uniform. It looks like the beginning of a bad porno movie but nothing more happens. She pokes at him with her club and, alarmed, he gets back in line. He whispers something to his wife in German, "Unglaublich" he hears, and she unbottons her brown shirt and pulls it down over her shoulders so that her pale breasts can be seen swelling above her light purple bra.

After an hour they reach the corner only to see the line develop into a snail shell. The fat woman in the uniform stands there allowing people into the labyrinth in clusters as she grunts loudly and makes irritable facial expressions. Things can't move fast enough. They are going over to wait in another line for several hours. A loudspeaker blurbs automated frequent warnings that it is not permissible to make humoristic or unsuitable remarks during the security check. It may cost you time in prison or deportation at your own expense. Humor is the first thing that disappears when a nation is at war, he thinks, but doesn't say out loud. During a previous visit he was just about to get into trouble after having made some jokes about bomb threats, and that was even before 9/11. Since then he has gotten better at keeping quiet. Though every so often he'll still whisper a few curses to himself.

He notices the surveillance camera panning the hallway with an almost inaudible humming sound.

Through a skylight he can see that it's grown dark outside. He has been waiting for over two hours now and the line has completely stopped moving. It smells like old sweat and bad breath. Once in a while an exaggerated aroma of cheap perfume will emerge. The air is completely static. At one point he sees an elderly woman take a perfume bottle from her bag and discreetly spray herself on one of her wrists. She is wearing a dusty rose-colored jogging outfit, a cheap gold necklace and white sneakers. She smiles back at him so that he can see her all-too-perfect teeth.

He is thinking about the summerhouse in Sweden. Of the family trips there, of a tuned-up scooter, of the silence, the mosquitoes and the blueberry pies. He thinks about his brother who sometimes reminds him of Jørgen Stein's big brother, Otto. For some inexplicable reason he thinks about a shopping trip to Obs in the shopping mall.

When it's finally his turn at the booth he is told that it is the wrong one. He should have been standing in the line furthest to the right the man behind the booth says, smiling apologetically. He tries to appeal to the man: he has been standing in line for over two hours and he smells like a goat. It wasn't necessary to mention that, but he does nevertheless and the passport officer nods sympathetically. He throws his passport over to a colleague and nods encouragingly, a friendly face that dares make a personal decision. The passport officer understands his argument which is indicated through his nod, his sad situation and his powerlessness. He can help him.

And the arrival could have ended at this point had it not been for the passport attendant's superior who at that very moment steps forth from the shadows and enters the story holding his pistol butt with a firm grip. "Is there a problem here?" he asks, his face pink from an accumulated lack of initiative. He fills out the entire uniform he is wearing. The material around the buttons is stretched to the limit to keep the shirt from ripping apart and the belt, hooked on the very last hole, cuts into the fat of his stomach, making it bulge out above his pants.

"Is there a problem here?" he repeats louder this time as he looks up at him, his eyes squinting.

"I accidentally stood in the wrong line," he says.

"Well, you'd better get in the right one then" the boss says in a stern voice. "And fast," he adds.

"But I've already spent over two hours waiting in line. I was just standing in the wrong one. It's not fair that I should have to stand in line twice as long as the others because no one informed me which line I was supposed to be in." He himself can hear that it sounds a little shrill.

"Now, you'd better watch out, sir."

"For what?"

"I'm warning you!"

"About what?"

"Would you be so kind as to follow me?" It doesn't sound like a question. The superior has unbuckled the clasp to his revolver and signals that he is prepared to use it if he doesn't follow him immediately. He nods insistently toward a door close to where they are and gives him a firm shove in the same direction. He looks around at the line for possible witnesses but everyone is either looking at the ground or looks at him reproachfully. The boss points toward the door. He shrugs his shoulders and walks in front of him to the door. He senses the line letting out a sigh of relief as he does so.

The room behind the door is small and modestly furnished: two chairs and a small square table. The superior pushes him around a little in the room. He has taken out his club and nudges him, grazes his genitals several times as he makes derogatory comments about his country, his appearance, his manlihood. His body ripples under his uniform and his face has turned a darker shade of red.

He imagines that he is lost in the desert. He imagines the burning sand. He imagines that he can see the mountains and a caravan moving up and down through the cliffs on its way there, perhaps even a rattlesnake that slithers across the sand.

"Have you been drinking?" the superior asks him.

"No."

"Have you taken any drugs?"

"No."

"Why are you acting so irrationally?"

"I didn't realize that I was."

"Are you starting on that again?"

"I'm sorry!"

"We take security very seriously in this country. I can send you straight back to where you came from if I determine that you pose a threat in any way to this country."

"I wouldn't want that, sir."

"That's better." He looks at him for a long time, as though assessing his potential danger. "Can I send you back out to the queue now without risking that you do something stupid?"

"Yes."

"Yes, sir."

"Yes, sir."

He lightens up a little. "The same rules apply to everyone in this country, you know. It is a de-mo-cra-cy," he says the last word with great emphasis. "It's no use that we only bend the rules for some, as much as we would like to help."

"No, sir."

Deep down he knows that in this world the superiors always decide. Within these four walls and a little beyond, it's just a matter of getting through this as smoothly as possible. To swallow one's pride and submissively play along. Outside the four walls the superior is nothing, he has no real education, no culture whatsoever, a bad salary and ugly clothes, but the unique thing about the US is that the system backs him up fully, as long as he does his job. There is no possibility to file a complaint, the superior has no superiors.

As a consequence, the superior is on top. He is on a total power trip at being able to decide and lord it over the upcoming corporates of this world who so desperately want to enter his country. Who fall to their knees over the ideologies of his nation and its superior materialism, just begging for fourteen days' asylum so they can get a glimpse of how life really ought to be lived. But the superior guards the entrance with a meticulous jealousy, oh yes he does. Paradise isn't accessible for the many, actually only for the few.

The superior is silently typing something on the computer, occasionally he sips cold coffee from a paper cup and has apparently forgotten that he is not alone. He presses "enter" and nods authoritatively as he finally looks up at him.

"You'll get by with a warning this time," he says.

"Thank you."

"I'll escort you back to the line."

They leave the room and pass through a closed booth back to the original line that, if possible, is even longer than the first one.

"Here you are," says the superior, leaving him there.

He looks around at the new line that begins a few meters to the right of the one he was in first. He counts to one hundred to himself with closed eyes. He imagines he is running in a marathon, the lactic acids, the cheerful band playing along the way, his friends accompanying him on their bikes. He imagines that he is lying on a beach in Rio. He imagines dinosaur tracks going directly up a cliff. He imagines he is having sex with the young blonde woman standing a few meters in front of him. While her parents and the superior are watching.

Five hours later he makes a finger print for the man behind the booth, goes through the interrogation and is photographed. He has dark circles under his eyes and unsavory skin. He admits everything. He is going to teach at a university in this shithole of a country which he wouldn't mind bombing at the first opportunity given him. "Welcome to the US," the man behind the booth says. He looks tired.

Angelina's Bottom

He collects his travel documents: his passport, his visa, the temporary residency permit, the letters from the university, the permit and the custom's receipt. Whereupon he nods to the tired custom's worker and enters the US with a few steps. The customs officer is once again standing in the shadow behind the counter and monitoring the room. He doesn't respond to his greeting.

He follows a Japanese family who have been looking around helplessly and have finally managed to ask the customs officer in cumbersome English sentences which direction they should now go. He points to the right and nods curtly. Together they pass a group of security officers who check their entry papers and send them through a metal detector. On the opposite end an impersonal hallway leads them further on. There are still no signs to be seen but at least there are other travelers they can cling to. He says something in English to the Japanese family and they hiss through their teeth. He assumes it is an expression of politeness in their culture and they continue walking in silence. He gives up trying to find a bathroom even though he actually really needs to take a pee. He looks around constantly but at no time does he come across the iconic symbol for a needy man and so is therefore forced to concentrate on not peeing in his pants. Paradoxically, the USA still uses DOS, he thinks, while most of the rest of the world has gone over to Windows a long time ago. In the US you've got to know the codes in order to navigate things while in Europe you get everything served to you with compassionate icons on a prettily designed silver spoon. Look! A picture of a garbage can. What do you think you put in it and are you certain you want to delete these files? Permanently? He considers telling that to the Japanese family in order to lighten the mood a little, but he gives up when he sees their forthcoming smiles. You only look that cheerful if you don't fathom a thing.

The luggage belt is standing still when they finally manage to find it. His luggage has been placed in a corner and he helps the Japanese family find theirs. His is salmon-colored and easy to spot, while theirs is still rotating further down on the conveyor belt. There is a note explaining that his luggage was selected for inspection, so it has been opened, and the airport apologizes if it looks messy. It was done in order to ensure that air space remains safe and to protect the nation. There is a reference to an article in the Patriot Act.

He crumbles the paper before throwing it into the garbage. He refuses to get worked up about it. All he wants right now is to get to a hotel and into bed. He refuses to get worked up. He thinks back to his time as a dishwasher, the plates he looked forward to smashing when he finally got off from work after far too long a night. The bike ride home along Strandvejen in the darkness.

He drags his luggage behind him through customs. It is heavy, and one of the wheels isn't rolling properly, but on the other hand he manages to make it through to the arrival hall without getting accosted. A couple of customs officers are standing around chit-chatting behind a low counter as they assess the new arrivals with squinting eyes. He opens the revolving doors out to the arrival hall and is just about to collide with a pretty girl who is standing with a sign with his name on it. At first he doesn't register it, but someway or other it must have sunk in after all because he addresses her.

"Hi," he says. "You're holding a sign with my name on it?"

"Welcome," she says, coolly. She must have been waiting for a long time.

"I'm sorry for the delay."

"No problem. You couldn't help it." There is still no emotion to be traced in her voice, but then again she doesn't sound entirely dismissive either. She looks pretty nice. She resembles a slightly chubby version of Angelina Jolie. She probably weighs about 8 kilos too much, but she has a pair of lively brown eyes and her lips are full.

Actually, he dreamed about Angelina Jolie on the plane. The overweight girl with the distant gaze must have awakened his subconscious. He dreamed about Clint Eastwood lying in his underwear next to Angelina Jolie. It wasn't exactly sexy underwear but he is, after all, an older man, you can't expect him to follow every single fashion trend that happens to come along, so it was a pair of old-fashioned underwear with a fly and a brown wedge. The two of them were in a photo shoot and Angelina had to caress Clint Eastwood's stomach. Which she did rather convincingly.

Suddenly he himself was part of the dream. He lay where Clint Eastwood had been lying except it wasn't him. He had become an odd sort of hybrid, stopped in the middle of the metamorphosis, with his own consciousness, in someone else's body, but he didn't question it and gave it very little thought, because he was now lying next to Angelina Jolie and the camera team had disappeared. She looked gorgeous. She wasn't wearing any clothes and lay halfway under a light duvet. He himself was only wearing Clint Eastwood's underwear and Angelina caressed his stomach as though he were still him and his hands explored her body. She was indescribably soft. Unfortunately he was afraid that his wife might come in and catch him by surprise together with Angelina. On the other hand, he was ready to get a divorce if it meant getting a blow job from those lips or being allowed to continue caressing her a little more on her back and buttocks. He was in a dilemma. His wife seemed to be on a space voyage; sometimes he was able to see her spaceship through the window but then she still managed to tear the door open and he jumped out of bed wrapped in the duvet, looking like an apologetic school boy. Angelina just smiled sweetly.

When he woke up the stewardess was busy removing his tray with the empty plastic wrap. She scrutinized him. He could still feel Angelina's soft buttocks in his hands and he looks up at her as she walks in front of him in a cheaper incarnation. Her soft bottom in a pair of jeans that are slightly too tight.

"Where are you taking me?" he asks.

"I've rented a car. When I realized how delayed you were going to be, I thought that might be the best thing. That way we're not dependent on public transportation."

"That was good thinking."

"Thanks."

Was there a little irony in her voice?

"Who has in fact sent you? I had no idea I was going to get picked up."

"The University, I think. I was only told to pick you up. I don't know much more than that."

An Angelic Light

The car is a Ford Mustang from 1967, a convertible with an eight-cylindered engine. It is red. The girl who sort of looks like Angelina Jolie is already sitting in it. "Jump in," she says, smiling sweetly. He puts his baggage in the small trunk, slams it shut and jumps into the front seat without opening the door. It's almost like in a movie, except he hits his knee against the steering wheel and can't get the car started. "You just have to rev it up," the girl says.

"What's your name?"

"Angelina."

He revs it up as he turns the key and the car starts with a roar that echoes across the parking lot. He puts it into gear and rolls underneath the open barrier and out onto the street. Angelina gives directions, pointing left and right with her soft fingers as the mild evening air tousles her long hair.

There aren't that many other cars out on the road. They are in the periphery of Houston, wide streets with poor asphalt and a traffic light every once in awhile that's far too slow at changing. The homeless sit on pieces of cardboard along the road, or on worn blankets, holding bottles wrapped in brown paper bags. One of them claps and laughs when he sees the convertible. The others are mostly preoccupied with themselves or the practical chores of the day, coffee that needs to be made and bread that has to be eaten. One place gives a portion of soup in an iron pot and he almost feels like stopping and asking if he can get a bowl. It looks pretty cozy. A bowl of soup and then a nap in the ditch with Angelina as a cushion. She even smells a little bit like detergent and looks so enticing and soft. It's easy to envision one's tired head on top of her stomach.

"Could you pull over, there?" she asks, pointing to a big sign that indicates it's a supermarket. "I could eat a bag of nachos."

"You bet," he says, as the dream bursts like a speech bubble above his head.

He shifts down to second gear, signals and looks over his shoulder even though a bicycle in these parts would truly be a sensation. Then he turns into the parking lot and finds a spot close to the entrance.

"Perfect," says Angelina and gets out of the car.

He turns off the engine and is immediately overwhelmed by the silence. He leans back and shuts his eyes. Some crickets are singing intensely in some trees in the far distance, but other than that there isn't a single sound to be heard until a truck the size of a city bus starts its engine in one of the rows behind them.

He gets out of the car and follows Angelina who has already started to walk toward the shop at this very moment under a gigantic neon sign upon which it says "Here Everything Is Better." Modesty isn't exactly the Americans greatest virtue. Angelina calls him from the door and he waves back. The light from the inside falls on her and she looks totally unreal, beautiful, with an angelic light around her head. Then she turns to the side, her slightly oversized bottom, and he discerns a big "M" for McDonald's on the other side.

Heroes

"Come home a hero" it says on some big signs that are hanging from the ceiling near the entrance. If you buy the right products in jumbo size, like ice cream, Coca Cola and popcorn, the family will greet you as a hero when you get home. He looks around. There are many heroes in the US, he concludes, and they are gaining weight like no one else is on earth. This is actually the world's most overweight town and people as fat as blue whales are shuffling around in jogging suits and in specially designed shoes, doing their shopping in humongous shopping carts to later get assistance to load it over in their pick-up trucks by the underpaid Mexican cashiers.

"Hey, wait for me!" he calls out, but Angelina disappears, being familiar with the lay-out of the store, behind one of the rows with a big shopping cart. He follows her, past the plastic statue of Ronald McDonald bidding him welcome with his arm raised and a big smile on his red clown mouth.

Angelina is standing in front of the shelves with breakfast items. She has taken a package down from the shelf and is turning it in her hand. "Do you like these?" she asks and tosses the package to him.

"I didn't know we were having breakfast together," he says, and she smiles. A sweet smile. "But I have no idea whether I like them. They look good to me. As long as they don't contain any cinnamon."

"You can choose some different ones, if you want."

He looks despondently up at the aisle with packages and extends his hand. She nods with pride. She can see that he is impressed with the selection.

"That's what democracy is all about," she says, smiling again. "Freedom to choose." He chooses not to comment on that. Instead he looks at the uniform boxes, the table of contents that predominantly lists what they don't contain: sodium, sugar, carbohydrates. When he looks up Angelina has disappeared and he finds her in front of the aisle with nachos. She has already managed to fill up the shopping cart with food products and now she is steering it with slight difficulty toward the cashier at the end of the supermarket where the smiling female and male cashiers are waiting to serve them.

"So how are you all doing, today?" they ask with expressionless smiles to everyone who approaches their checkout counter, "Paper or plastic?" and "It sure is hot today," perhaps a few compliments about the screaming children in the shopping cart, the washed out clothes, or one's dialect if you've really bought a lot or are fumbling with the payment.

They place the items on the conveyor belt.

"Are you taking it?" Angelina asks.

"Yes," he says halfway to her, but addresses the male cashier, it's certainly nice weather today and pays. It's not so expensive which, on the other hand, may mean he'll get something later in return, he thinks, assuming he has made a deposit for a round of pussy, things need to balance out, that much he's learned.

He pushes the shopping cart out to the car, past Ronald McDonald and the wrong way through the entrance door. An elderly lady with blue hair is forced to stagger a few steps sideways in order to avoid getting hit. The cart is also hard to steer because one of the wheels keeps going berserk. It constantly wants to go to the right and he curses coarsely: at the country, at Angelina, at himself and that goddamn shopping cart.

The wheel on that goddamn shopping cart. Still, he manages to get to the car where he unloads the items on the small back seat. He doesn't have the energy to open the trunk. He's very tired.

"So," he says with feigned cheerfulness, "We should be able to manage for the next few hours or so."

"Hmm."

He pushes the shopping cart into the empty parking space while Angelina starts the car. He sees that it continues rolling but he doesn't care. He jumps into the front seat and they drive out onto the road. In the rear view mirror he can see the shopping cart continue as it collides with a big pick-up truck and he hears a car alarm go off. He ducks. Like in a movie. Angelina shakes her head and hits the accelerator so they disappear into the horizon. Seen from behind: the red backside of the car that grows smaller and smaller, Angelina's fluttering hair, the sound of the powerful engine on its way away and his silhouette that turns up further down the road. He runs a hand through his hair and leans back.

They continue down the road in silence. He turns on the radio and finds a country music station. It's the only station that comes through clearly but it also matches the mood in the car, the mild evening air, the humming of the engine and the road that disappears underneath them. He has noticed that the rhythm is tuned according to the stripes on the road at 80 km an hour.

"Try driving a little slower," he says but she misunderstands his intention and thinks he wants to start deciding things.

"No," she responds. Defiantly.

"But I just want to see whether the stripes match up with the music." She looks at him without saying anything and he looks back. He wants to explain it better but he can't find any other way of putting it so he gives up. He would also like to find a different topic of discussion but he is at a complete loss. On the other hand, his ears are creaking and his head feels a little hazy after the flight. He feels he owes it to her to be a little entertaining so he places his hand on the backside of the seat, grazing her hair on the way. She looks at him suspiciously but smiles when she sees the expression on his face. He interprets her smile as an invitation and carefully caresses her cheek, moves a strand of hair from her eye and pushes it behind her ear. She shuts her eyes. He places his hand on her thigh. She looks at him with a new glow in her eyes. Desire? He carresses her throat and shoulders. She lets him do it. He caresses her breasts. Her nipples grow hard beneath the thin material of her shirt. His hand glides down toward her lap. She signals and pulls over.

They park at a rest area and have sex. He is considering how she'd prefer to have it and tries making it look like a porno movie, up against the Mustang, but it doesn't work, he thinks, and he spends far too much time considering what she's thinking and whether perhaps he may have gotten a little too fat? She is quite firm. It's not how it ought to be, and she looks a little ridiculous, bending over his cock, or with her breasts crushed flat against the engine hood. Shouldn't it feel better than this? Shouldn't it satisfy something other than his immediate desire, and what about afterward? How will he feel in a short while after he has emptied himself inside of her, or would it be better if he came all over her instead, and he doesn't get much further than that because he comes before he manages to conclude his thought, and his member immediately shrinks and turns far too little, plops out of her, and then suddenly they are just standing there, looking at each other with a dull expression in their eyes?

They put on their clothes in silence without looking at each other. It's not a noteworthy silence and yet it is loaded with a tad of embarrassment . From not knowing what the other is thinking and not feeling comfortable with the sense of insecurity.

There are some garbage cans next to the parking spots and an animal is busy rummaging through one of them. It's too dark to see what sort of animal it is but it could be a squirrel or a marten.

Every so often a car drives by on the road and the car lights sweep across them and a ways up into the air, lighting the top of the electric poles in a glimpse of light. Thanks to some low bushes along the road they are not visible.

He can hear that Angelina has opened the trunk. She is rustling with some bags and goes over to him. He looks at the sky with an empty sensation in his stomach. She stands next to him. Perhaps she is also looking up at the sky, the stars that are exceptionally clear. He can hear her opening a bag, and shortly afterward he can smell the spicy aroma of nachos with chili and paprika.

"Want some?" she asks, nudging him gently with her elbow. He pulls home his gaze back from the stars and looks at her. If only she'd shut up, he thinks.

"Want some?" she repeats, as she looks at him with pleading eyes. Are you angry? they ask, and he hurries up and responds as neutrally as possible. He doesn't have the energy for an emotional confrontation, and he isn't angry, at the most tired and slightly sad that it didn't feel better. He doesn't say that nor that he regrets having wasted his approaching guilty conscience on bad sex.He is already thinking in American, he notes, a guilty conscience as a commodity for good sex. He brushes her hair away from her left cheek and pushes it in back of her ear, and she leans against him. He can feel her breasts against his ribs which end up giving him a little tingling sensation in his midriff after all. They stand like that for a little while before he disrupts the quietness and the romantic mood that is about to be built up again, completely contrary to his intentions.

"Maybe we should continue driving?" he asks.

"Yes."

Two Elderly Men

He must have fallen asleep. He remembers them driving a ways in the darkness. That the sultry wind blew in his face, the never-ending road's rhythmical stripes in the cone of light before them and the sounds of the night behind the noise of the engine. That he lay looking at Angelina's profile, her Greek nose and clear forehead. He has always had a thing for strong women and he grows completely weak in the knees if they know how to drive, too. He remembers her bending over and turning on the radio and changing stations and then changing stations again. But then he must have fallen asleep.

He is struggling to awaken. He senses that they have stopped and he opens his heavy eyelids. He has been awake for almost 48 hours and his eyes are swollen sore. He just manages to see that Angelina is talking with two elderly men. They have stopped at a gas station and she is busy filling up the car with one foot resting on the bumper. He can see her in the rear view mirror. If he moves his head a little he can also see the men. One is wearing a leather cap and has a small mustache. The other is a handsome, gray haired man wearing a sports jacket. He looks nice. The last thing he sees before having to shut his eyes again is the gray haired man pointing at him with a walking cane as he says something to the other two who smile. He can hear their subdued voices for awhile after he has shut his eyes. "My murderer," he hears at one point, but then it seems to get all mixed up with a dream in which the man with the mustache is Hitler having sex with Angelina up against the car as the man with the cane watches with interest.

MOTEL

ngelina signals and slows down the speed of the car. He doesn't know for how long they've been driving but he senses that it's been quite a while. He has been sleeping, yet most of the time he has been in a strange state between sleeping and being awake in which Hitler and a nice looking elderly gentleman can have sex with his driver without it seeming suspiciously unreal.

There still aren't many cars on the road. They've driven through some small towns a few times, a number of traffic lights, neon signs and billboards, but there hasn't been a soul in sight. Only once does he see a group of people cross the road and as they drive past he notices that they are coming out of a church. This is the Bible Belt and it truly is tight-fitting around the waists of most of the inhabitants.

"-otel" it says on an old neon sign under which they are driving. The "M" has disappeared, but its contours are casting a faint light into the darkness. Angelina is steering the car toward the building and turns off the engine, making the silence wash over them. They sit still for a little while, staring out into space. As though they had agreed to wait with getting out of the car. The sound of the engine continues in his mind, the stripes, when he shuts his eyes and leans his head back.

"I thought maybe we could sleep here," says Angelina.

"Where are we?"

"Not too far from the University but it's too late to check in there. Besides, I'm too tired to do any more driving."

"That's fine, I really need to get some sleep now." He looks around toward the reception faintly lighting up in the darkness to the right of them in the far distance. How am I ever going to make it there? he thinks.

They get out and walk over to the reception. Angelina stops and takes hold of his arm.

"Doesn't that resemble a painting by Edward Hopper?" she asks, and it actually does, but he catches himself being surprised by the fact that she is familiar with Hopper.

"To a T."

"I studied art at community college a few years ago," she says, as though sensing what he is thinking.

"Hopper was one of my favorites."

"Also mine. No one can capture the mood in the US like him."

"He's even managed to capture the crickets," she says, smiling.

It's close to midnight, he realizes, when he checks his wrist watch, a fine, older make with a leather band he has inherited from his father. They have disengaged themselves from the picture and have gone over to the reception where an overweight guy is sitting and sleeping across the counter. They can see him through the window. He is lying with his chin splattered out across a super hero cartoon, bathed in a soft light from the lamp hanging from the ceiling. It looks like an aquarium, the kind that one always finds in a doctor's waiting room, with a few fish in a dull rectangle of water, without any unnecessary plants or toys. All you can see is one fish at the bottom of the aquarium which Angelina awakens when she opens the door, letting some of the light in from the parking lot.

The guy awakens with a grunt. A bell makes a short clang and it sounds exactly as it should, the sound of the American provinces. It could have been a gas station with wooden shelves and a meager selection of goods, a cheap restaurant, or a motel with small unpretentious rooms and a worn down reception like this one where the guy sits up in his chair and looks at them in surprise. As though he knows them and can't believe they have finally arrived. But then the expression on his face fades and he lowers his shoulders, subdues a yawn and makes do with looking tired.

It is hard to guess his age, but he may possibly be older than he looks. In his twenties, he guesses, but he isn't sure which half, and he could also be in his early thirties. He is wearing a checkered shirt and a brown cardigan that doesn't suit him. His hair is thin and combed to the side in an unfortunate parting. In his mid thirties? He has a name tag. Philip is his name and he is the manager of the place.

"I'm sorry," he says with a drawl and gets up. "How can I help you?"

"We need two rooms," says Angelina.

It looks as though Philip is suppressing a smile. As though there is something funny about the situation that the rest of us have missed. Perhaps it's just insecurity. Or a failed attempt to seem forthcoming.

"I'm afraid I only have one left," he says. He looks up at the key rack behind him from which only one key is hanging.

"Really?" Angelina asks. "There are only three cars in the parking lot."

Philip gives her a tired look. "That may be, but I have only one room left."

It is quiet for a moment. He looks over at Angelina.

"Do you want it?" Philip asks.

"Of course we do," Angelina answers sharply. "Thank you."

She fills out the papers while he considers whether the animal at the rest-area could have been a raccoon. He thinks about her breasts crushed flat against the engine hood and he is thinking about whether they are going to have sex in the room when they wake up. He is thinking of his wife back home and the children she wants.

"I think that's about it," says Philip. "Is it okay if I write that you are married? So as not to get into trouble with the authorities?"

"That's fine," Angelina quickly says.

"May I offer you a drink before you turn in? It's custom for us to offer one to couples who stay the night."

Before they have a chance to answer, he has placed a gold tray on the counter. There are already a couple of small glasses containing a whitish liquid, plus an egg cup with sesame seeds.

"Help yourselves," he insists.

"Thank you." He casts a sidelong glance at her but she lifts her glass, giving them a toast. Philip pours himself a glass from a bottle hidden behind some folders under the counter. They drink and he dips his finger in the sesame seeds. They taste like bird seed. He remembers the taste from when he had a bird as a child. A budgie that stood above the television and ended up going insane.

"It's a traditional local drink," says Philip. "Its based on fermented yams and local herbs. Together with the seeds it symbolizes the fertility of the soil in this area."

"It tastes good," he says, looking down into the glass. "Thank you for the drink."

"I thought it would be a nice tradition to introduce you to. Anyway," he hesitates,"I don't want to keep you guys up any longer. Just cross the parking lot whenever you're ready. Your room is over there," he says, pointing out the window. "If you need anything just holler."

They go back to the car in silence. He takes his luggage out of the trunk and looks at his key. For a long time. Suddenly Philip is standing next to him although he can't really explain how he managed to sneak up on him like that without him discovering it. "Do you want me to help you with your luggage?"

Angelina is gone, he realizes, and in an attempt to forestall the embarrassing mood that is already beginning to build up, he mumbles, "I'm coming now," in the direction of their room.

"She has already gone to bed, I believe," Philip says dryly. "It's been quite a while now. I wondered why you remained standing for so long after she had gone. So I thought I better go out and make sure everything was alright."

"Thanks."

"But then I could hear you were snoring. That you were standing there snoring."

Philip's mouth smells like sleep. Sleep and old coffee, he detects, when he yawns without turning his head away. He doesn't dare think about how he himself smells.

"It's been a long day," he says explanitorily in order to break the silence. His voice sounds all wrong in the darkness, strangely faint, and continues to linger in the mild air in the parking lot.

Philip doesn't say anything, just stands observing him with his fixed smile.

"I can imagine," he finally says. He is standing somewhat restlessly, as though he wants to say something more but instead straightens his sparse hair with his fingers spread like a comb and clears his throat.

"Don't you want me to help you with your piece of luggage?" he then repeats. He looks him in the eyes as he asks and can see that it is a line he has practiced and that he had to force himself to say it. He clearly prefers looking at people's torsoes or the lower part of their faces but he has confidence-inspiring eyes even though the smile that is stuck to his mouth isn't to be found in them. On the other hand, he seems to have a nervous tic around his eye, well, maybe not exactly a tic, but something similar.

"That's really not necessary. I'm awake now, thanks

anyway, I think I'll just go to bed as fast as possible."

Philip bends down awkwardly in front of him and takes his luggage before he has a chance to react. "I insist," he says, unfolding his chronic smile.

He follows him toward the door behind which, he presumes, Angelina has fallen asleep. He imagines tossing his clothes off and crawling down to her under the covers. He goes through the process mentally. Sometimes he gets stuck because he doesn't know where to start but it really shouldn't be all that complicated: he imagines pulling off his clothes and going to bed. He doesn't have the energy to brush his teeth.

In front of him Philip has stopped walking. He places the suitcase on the ground and turns around. "Would you like to see something before you lie down?" he asks. "I know it sounds like a strange question at this time of day. But it'll only take a moment."

"I'm really beat."

"So am I, but I really need to show you something. It won't take more than a moment," he repeats decisively. He must have nodded because Philip picks up the suitcase again and walks in the direction of a small shed a little ways to the right of them. He had noticed it when they arrived and thought that it mostly resembled a sentry box, a sort of shelter for a guard, but now he sees that it more resembles a tool shed. At any rate, Philip stops in front of it, puts down the suitcase and takes out a bunch of keys from his pocket. He unlocks the door and disappears into the shed but appears shortly afterward and motions his guest to come closer as he takes the suitcase in with him. Then the door shuts behind him.

He stands for a brief moment and looks around. The parking lot is vacant. Not a single person has passed them on the road. The otel-sign sends a crackling light in his direction but other than that it is completely dark. Except for the sign and the exceptionally bright stars lighting up the sky in tiny blurry dots. Philip must have turned off the light in the reception when he went out to his snoring guest.

Some crickets are buzzing a little further away in the low bushes behind the parked cars, and the motel's air conditioning is humming loudly. There are some big compressors down at the bottom of the staircase, he sees.

He doesn't really know what to do with himself. The whole thing seems unreal in an oddly real way. A thin-haired guy who disappears inside a shed with his suitcase at a parking lot in the late hours in Texas, the crickets that are still singing, the "-otel" sign's crackling. He takes out a nighttime cigarette from his pants pocket, lights it with a useless disposable lighter and takes a deep drag. Then he walks over to the shed.

Spiral Staircases

"Unfortunately you're not allowed to smoke in here," says Philip when he has entered the shed. He looks at him in disbelief but takes a last puff, opens the door, and tosses the cigarette out into the darkness.

"I'm sorry, but those are the rules."

"Of course."

The shed is slightly bigger on the inside than it appeared to be from the outside, with a bench on one side and a wall-mounted shelf and a bunch of junk boxes on the other. It's hard to tell exactly what it was that so urgently needed to be shown that he had to be dragged over here in the middle of the night.

"Okay, fine," he mumbles, as Philip smiles slyly. He senses his irritation mounting but he manages to repress it. He is known for being patient, but sometimes it manages to pop up anyway, his impatience. Usually the irritation will manifest as irony or small sarcastic comments.

"Okay, wait'll you see this! You better put this on first. It could be both dirty and cold where we're going." He tosses a brown boiler suit to him.

"Do I really need to? I think your shed is impressive, but I really need to go to bed now. Can't you show me the rest tomorrow?"

"It'll only take a moment," Philip says for the third time. He bends down and moves a cheap rag rug, uncovering a trapdoor with a handle which he pulls up with great difficulty. "Hmmm," he moans when the trapdoor slides up, revealing a black hole.

"Wow, a hole."

"Not just a hole," Philip says, smiling, it takes a lot more than that to discourage him. He reaches down and turns on the light with a switch that isn't visible to him. But then a staircase appears of which you can only see the top steps. After that they dissolve into the darkness.

He doesn't know what to say.

"Put on that outfit," says Philip. He has sat down on the bench and is maneuvering with his own, trying to get his shoes through the pant legs. He has chosen not to take them off. Discouraged, he sits down next to him and removes his own before pulling on the suit. It fits perfectly. He zips it up, puts his shoes back on and they are both finished at the same time.

"What does the 'M' stand for?" he asks, pointing at

his chest upon which there is a green "M" printed with a circle around it.

"We'll get to that," says Philip. His eyes blink a little nervously. "Shall we?" he asks, pointing down the staircase.

He's got something with stairs. He once lived in a house in which there previously lived a blacksmith who specialized in spiral staircases. He had built several around the house which had three storeys. Two made of wood and metal and a third made of white bricks. Ever since he has had something with stairs. This one is made of metal, with holes in the steps so that you can look down into the darkness as you walk down them. Philip has already half disappeared. He can see his pale pate underneath the thin hair before he gets swallowed up by the darkness. He follows cautiously behind.

"Will you shut the trap door behind you?" Philip asks somewhere below him. "You can never be too careful."

"That's true." He reaches for the leather strap which is fastened on the underside of the trap door and pulls it closed behind him. He may have been irritated before, but now he's worried. It must be due to the sound of the trap door closing. He looks down in search of Philip, but he can't see him. For a moment he considers opening the trap door and going in the opposite direction, but for one thing it would feel like a failure after he just voluntarily closed it, and for another his curiosity has, despite everything, been awakened. And for a third thing, he is too tired to make an active decision, it's easier just to keep following.

He's taken another three steps when the darkness below him disappears. Some neon tubes are flashing to finally cast a clinical light across the staircase and the whitewashed hallway below it. The staircase bends in several places on the way down so as not to take up so much space in the room. A spiral staircase! He thinks more cheerfully.

"Isn't this better?" Philip shouts. He is standing at the bottom of the staircase smiling up at him.

He instinctively looks up when he finally reaches the bottom. It's an impressive room, with whitewashed walls bathed in the cold light of the neon lights. Church-like, he thinks but why should the Church have a patent on big, white rooms? In front of them the narrow ceiling and walls wind into one another and continue as a high-ceilinged passage. Like a cervix, he imagines and Philip is standing at the very spot where the uterus turns into a cervix. He turns and motions him to come closer before he continues into the darkness.

A Simple Individual
with Good Intentions

He has followed Philip down the hallway and through a door to the right. The hallway continues further ahead, but the neon lights stop working a ways inside, and from then on it lies in complete darkness.

The room turns out to be a small workshop of sorts. Along one of the walls there are some television screens on a long table on which are placed various tools. A screwdriver, a drill. Several spanners in different sizes. At the end is a laptop. Next to it are several cartoon magazines and a single book.

Philip turns on a switch and the room wakes up with a humming sound, the screens flash, a printer hawks and spits and the air conditioning starts up.

Pictures of the motel's rooms appear on the screens. Philip points at one of them furthest to the left where he catches sight of Angelina who is lying under a white sheet and sleeping. She doesn't look pretty, but who does when they are sleeping? Her mouth is open and some saliva is running down her cheek. On one of the screens a woman is putting on clothes after having apparently taken a bath, while a man is sitting reading the newspaper in his underwear on a third. It must be close to morning. Philip looks over at him in anticipation with a small uncertain smile.

"Is this legal?"

Philip looks at him before answering. He chooses his words carefully, he senses. His eyes look to the right to find the answers there and when he has found them he articulates them slowly and cautiously.

"I had hoped you wouldn't react in that way. I think that's a rather hypocritical point of departure," he says, smiling, "a know-all and somewhat condescending attitude you're demonstrating."

He's isn't quite certain how to respond. "You may be right about that," he says in order not to upset him further.

"I have, of course, considered doing what I felt was the right thing. I'm not doing it for my own sake, but in order to contribute toward creating a better world." He looks up at him and says more calmly, "There are certain things that are above the law, I believe. And how can I possibly monitor people's interactions with one another if I can't monitor them?"

"But don't you need ..."

Philip lifts his hand as though to signal that there is nothing more to discuss. He continues the motion by brushing the same hand through his hair. "If the government can do it, then why can't the individual whose intentions are noble do it?"

"That's of course one way to look at it." He senses that continuing the discussion is pointless. In the past he would have completed it, but he has grown pragmatic with age and he can see that fanaticism has covered Philip's eyes like a membrane. It's hard to explain but there is something about his gaze that makes him back out. Philip looks at him with interest and considers his silence before continuing, "It may sound a little strange but I've always wanted to be a hero. I've read about heroes ever since I was a boy and I seriously believe that it is every American's duty to strive to be one."

"And is it only Americans who can be heroes?"

"No, no. Of course not." He considers it for a moment. "But there is no other place in the world like America. We have endless opportunities. We can pursue any dream that pops into our minds."

"Interesting," he mumbles.

"I've always read cartoons. I learned to read by reading Superman, Batman and Spiderman. They were my best friends and biggest idols. It might sound like a cliché, but it's true."

"Really?" he says dully. He no longer knows what he is expected to answer.

"Are there any super heroes in Denmark?"

He hesitates. This is something he actually knows something about. But he doesn't know whether he has the energy to share his knowledge. He looks at Philip who is standing in anticipation and observing his stomach.

"Yes," he then says, "of course there are, but not in the same way as over here. The word 'helt', which he pronounces clearly in Danish, "actually derives from the Indo-European 'kalut' which means 'healthy' and 'beautiful' but which later came to mean 'courageous man.' He partook in a Scandinavian conference a while ago where he talked about the differences between American and Scandinavian world views. And in which he drew a comparison to the concept of the hero. "The concept defines itself in contrast to its antonym, which is 'anti hero' and 'villain,' that is, evil minded individuals who perform evil deeds."

Philip nods.

"But the concept is also in contrast to the trivial, the normal, mundane and day-to-day. Aside from the anti-hero, the villain, the monster. "He looks up to make sure that Philip is listening to him and he interprets it as an invitation to ask a question.

"How is that different from over here?"

"Over here the concept is defined more as being physical. Here, the hero is strong and good in war. His intellect doesn't play much of a role. The physical is above the mental, you could say. The intellect isn't suited to engage with this world, it belongs to the ivory tower, and is impractical and weak, while the body is assertive and efficient. It is a dogme which religion, for example, elaborates."

"Exciting," says Philip.

"Yes, I'd like to work more with it."

Philip scrutinizes him with his little smile.

"It must be fun seeing things from the outside. I prefer to be the hero while you would rather make do with observing him."

"I don't know whether 'make do' is the right choice of words."

"I'm sorry, I didn't mean to offend you." He looks around in the workshop in the silence that follows, blinks his eyes a little and brushes his hand through his hair.

"Do you want to see some more?" he asks, motioning toward the hallway.

"Why not?"

"Even though it'll get more dirty now?"

He frowns, but nevertheless follows Philip who goes back out to the hallway.

An Ominous Splash

They go out into the hallway and into the darkness to the right. He has to feel his way through, but he always hears Philip who comes with little comments and utterances in front of him. "Watch out here," he says, and "You have to duck a little there." At the end of the hallway they have to go down on their knees in order to get through a low ceilinged hallway with an arch.

"It was supposed to be used as a reservoir for the area," Philip partly shouts a good distance ahead of him, "but something went wrong, apparently there wasn't enough water so it was never put to use. It's connected to the sewer so you can really easily get around."

"Where are we going?"

"Well, it wouldn't really be a surprise if I told, now would it?" He sighs out loud. "You'll have to sit down here, and slide forward on your butt."

He can hear trickling water nearby, so he does as he is told. He hears Philip disappear with a small splash in front of him.

"Just come on," he says a ways below him, and he

slides a little further before the base disappears. Then tries to reach the water with his feet but ends up letting go and landing next to Philip. The water splashes up on his boiler suit.

"Way to go," he says acknowledgingly.

He can't tell whether he is smiling.

They slush along with the water reaching their knees. Neither of them say anything. He, because it's all much too overwhelming. Philip, because he's thinking.

"You sound a little like my father," he says after they have walked a ways in silence. His voice sounds different, but it may be the surroundings that have changed it. Some of the sound has to be lost in the curvature of the concrete wall, or be thrown back distortedly, he thinks. He sounds sad.

The water isn't cold, yet still he has started to freeze. He can also sense his asthma starting up. His chest constricts, and he automatically inhales deeply in order to expand it.

Philip doesn't say anything more. It's as though he expects him to defend himself. Or ask more detailed questions about his father. He waits for a moment, but nothing more is said.

"How did your father sound?"

"He is a professor at a university. He no longer lives with my mother, but I see him from time to time." He pauses again. "He sounded wise, was what I meant, but also somewhat like a know-it-all and preaching. I couldn't see that back then, but I've been thinking a lot about it of late. That he never listened to me. That he never took the time to learn anything about my world."

"In which case I'm sad to hear I sound like him. He doesn't sound all too sympathetic."

"You know nothing about that. He was. All I'm saying is that he never used to listen to me."

"You're right."

But now I'm going to show him that I am worth listening to."

"What is he professor of?"

He grows quiet. "I don't remember. Something to do with literature or art, or perhaps philosophy?"

"That sounds interesting."

Victory or Death

They continue in silence. His eyes have grown so used to the darkness at this point that he can discern the moving water and sometimes Philip in front of him. A few times he hears a couple of ominous splashes when something jumps from the wall or the adjacent sewers. Then Philip clears his throat.

"I remember one time when he was still living at home he told me the story of the Alamo ... I couldn't have been all that old because he moved when I was nine but I recall the story almost verbatim."

"It's a wonderful story."

"My father specifically told about the choice between staying and leaving, between being a hero and a coward. 'You choose what you want to do with your life yourself,' he said." Philip stops and turns toward him. Despite the darkness he can see that he has red eyes.

"That sounds right."

"The decisive moment during the defense of the Alamo arose when Travis drew a line in the sand," he bends down and illustrates the movement with his finger on the water, "and said that those who wanted to defend the fortress had to pass the line to him. Which they all did except for one."

"There has to be one left to illustrate the point," he adds, but Philip ignores him.

"It's significant that the men were forced to make an active decision," he continues unperturbed. "A hero doesn't remain standing in one place, he steps forth when fate calls him." No easy way out here, Travis thought, he thinks, the story condemns the slightest mistake harshly. But he was wrong. History constructs the truth according to one's taste.

Philip takes a few symbolic steps further in the sewer and points to the disappeared line in the water. "When Travis drew the line in the sand he had just received the news that the reinforcements wouldn't get there in time. The Mexicans were arming themselves outside the walls and Travis could with considerable certainty conclude that they were all going to die defending this mission fortress. He had sent an appeal to his countrymen in which he described his impossible situation, surrounded by thousands or more Mexicans under the leadership of the grim Santa Anna. He had already endured 24 hours of bombardment without losing a single man and the

American flag was still waving above the wall. He was, of course, not alone at the fort, but he was the one who kept their morale up and the Mexicans at bay. He is my great inspiration," says Philip.

"I can understand that. He was also a true hero."

"And I'm grateful that my father told me the story that night. It determined my destiny."

He passes the line in the water and Philip smiles approvingly to him. "Victory or death. Wasn't that how it went?"

"Exactly."

TIRED HEROES

Don't they ever get tired, those heroes? Or that flock of capitalistic fortune hunters who stole the land from Mexico? Rumors of Texas' wealth got Americans from near and far to travel there and when there were enough of them they initiated a rebellion against the government. Even the famous David Crockett heard about the endless possibilities in Texas and when he lost his seat in Congress, he packed up his family and traveled west. Up until the election he had told his constituents that he would continue to loyally serve them but if they didn't vote for him they could go to hell while he would go to Texas. Fate would have it that he ended up in San Antonio right when the Mexicans came and he lost his life in the battle for Alamo. That is: he survived the battle itself but was caught along with six others by General Castrillon and taken to Santa Anna. Crockett tried to talk his way out of the tough spot and asserted his innocence, he had been a mere tourist who had been taken prisoner in exchange of gunfire, but Santa Anna ordered that he and the others be executed on the spot. According to eyewitness accounts they were first tortured and mutilated before they were killed.

He knows the story from a lecture he once gave about the joys of Texas. David Crockett had gotten a certain reputation as a bear killer and story teller and the rumor won him a seat in Congress. He was of ordinary stock so he fulfilled all the criteria for a hero: a self-made man, courageous, assertive and intelligent. But if he already had a certain reputation before the Alamo, it veritably exploded afterward. He couldn't have wished for a better death.

Immediately after his death books and magazines dealing with his heroic deeds began to appear in great numbers. His diaries and almanacs were written and published and he became the main character in a number of films and books for children and adults with illustrative woodcuts depicting the adventurous events. Crockett killed buffaloes with his bare hands, shot Indians, evaded tornadoes on the back of lightning and saved America from freezing over by smearing the axis of the Earth with bear fat and kicking it off with a well-placed kick.

In a wonderful movie from 1960 about the Alamo, John Wayne plays David Crockett and dies heroically by exploding the ammunition room in a last desperate attempt to keep the Mexicans at bay. That's how a true hero dies, with his characteristic raccoon hat askew and a spiteful smile on his lips. When the film about Crockett came out, the price of raccoon tails subsequently rose by more than 2000%.

While he has been mentally absent, Philip has been trodding along further into the darkness. He hears his footsteps moving as in a dream.

In the most recent movie about the Alamo from 2000 Crockett is played by Billy Bob Thornton who has been married to Angelina Jolie. When they get divorced Billy Bob declared very diplomatically that he might just as well fuck a sofa as have sex with Angelina.

So much for the American hero.

An Iconic M

He can't see Philip and he can just barely discern his feet dragging in the water. He feels rather alone. He can really feel the water now, the rats, the stench and the creeping sense of claustrophobia of being below the ground. The boiler suit isn't much help. It reminds him of the time he was stuck in a foxhole under the ground and his sister had to pull him back up by his leg. The neighbor's son had lured him by saying that he probably didn't dare crawl down there. He himself had crawled down ahead of him and had placed a collective card and some poultry rings in the foxhole which he promised he would get if he dared fetch them. He ended up getting the poultry ring as a consolation prize for not tattle-tailing, but he lost them to the shoe maker's son the next day in the schoolyard.

He calls out into the darkness and he can hear the footsteps stopping in their tracks.

"Are you coming?" Philip calls back. A little while later he catches up with him. He considers making a comment about the absurdity of the situation. The danger of leaving him in a sewer he isn't familiar with but he doesn't feel like moralizing now, and anyway, there is something about the situation that doesn't allow it.

One of his hands seems to be bleeding, there is something red, at any rate, that is dripping from there down into the water. He has to wipe it in the boiler suit several times. He's been about to fall a few times, but then he's managed to save himself by placing one of his hands on the wall, and once on the slimy ground of the sewer.

"Are we there soon?"

"Where?" Philip asks in a hard voice, and he senses a chill go down his spine. He doesn't know whether it is a sneaking sense of insecurity or whether it's dripping from the ceiling. It dawns on him that he is entirely at the mercy of a strange man who apparently knows the tunnel in and out. They have to turn down smaller paths several times, and another time they have to get down on their knees to get over to a sewer that must run parallel with the one they were in. Every so often he catches a glimpse of Philip's brown boiler suit, but the water, the walls and the surroundings have disappeared once again into the darkness. He would never be able to find his way back alone.

They walk a little further until the sound of their shuffling feet suddenly stops and he discovers that they are moving upward. The water disappears below them, presumably runs through a grid further ahead as they step upwards a sloping chute. He can see light ahead, and he imperceptibly relaxes his shoulders. Philip turns around to make sure he is still following him. "Wait'll you see this," he says as he motions ahead with his hand.

A Bulge in the Hallway

The room is like a bulge in the hallway. You may envision a snake that's devoured a hamster. The walls are arched, so it is reminiscent of a cupola and there is some light coming from a source above which he can't catch sight of even if he tilts back his head and tries.

The room is fairly austerely arranged. Along one of the walls there is a file cabinet from an earlier time, and along the other a big writing desk with a computer and various messy things, some pizza boxes, empty plastic cups and cans. In the middle of the room there are two black leather armchairs with built-in foot stools and a dated refrigerator that can make ice cubes. At the end of the wall there is a ladder that leads nowhere.

"Want a soda?" Philip asks as he opens the fridge.

He nods.

"With ice cubes?"

"No thank you." He learned that a long time ago. The ice cubes take up all the space in the cup and water down the taste. Furthermore, they taste like chlorine. Only an idiot would choose to have ice cubes.

Philip hands him the can of soda and sits down in one of the armchairs. He follows behind and sits down next to him, flips the chair back and shuts his eyes.

"Quite a place you've got here."

"Yeah, thanks. I'm not the one who's built the whole thing but I've arranged it so it suits my needs. I've thrown out quite a lot of things."

He looks over at Philip and makes a toast toward him with the can.

"Will you now tell me what the M stands for?" he says, pointing to his chest.

"I think it's a little embarrassing. But I had to come up with a name, a kind of super hero's name. So I took the most obvious: Motel-guy. That's what the world will know me as."

"Then there's no use in being embarrassed about it."

They sit still with their eyes closed.

"I think it's a good name," he then says.

He is just about to fall asleep when Philip pokes him.

"I thought I should show you where you are," he says. "I've just gotten a program installed that works as a kind of simulator. Something along the lines of Google

Earth but just a lot more advanced. Don't ask how it works, it just does."

He has fetched a laptop which he is sitting with in his lap and turned on a projector pointing at the wall at the end of the room. He has taken down the ladder so that the picture won't have to wind around it. He double clicks with the mouse on an icon that resembles a helicopter.

"It's sort of like having your own helicopter," he explains. "Or like being able to fly yourself."

"The program opens and suddenly they are in the motel's reception, where he and Angelina a short while ago surprised the sleeping guy who is now sitting next to him and with great precision is grazing his finger across the mouse pad. They go out the door.

"Impressive," he says, impressed. He has sat up in the chair in order to better be able to see it.

"Yes, I've installed the cameras myself in the reception, the rest has been pieced together by satellite recordings and live cameras set at various places. There are a huge number, and they cover 96.7% of Texas. I myself have put some of them up but that's mostly to get better views of places that are already covered."

They walk a little bit around the parking lot in front of the motel. They open the door to Angelina's room. She is still sleeping.

"Some of it is animated." Philip says. "We aren't opening the door to reality, of course, but it gives the illusion of an extra dimension, I think."

"It's extremely life-like," he says. "Can you get any closer?"

"Of course." They go closer. Angelina turns in her sleep under the duvet and he can clearly see her soft buttocks, even one of her nipples as she remains lying halfway on her back.

"Can you lift the duvet?" He would like to lie next to her right now. How did he even end up here in the first place? He suddenly can't recall the causal connection but he knows he must have made a couple of wrong decisions along the way.

"Wait a second! That wasn't what I actually wanted to show you," says Philip. He steers them back out the door, out to the parking lot where he sees his car parked a ways from Angelina's room. Then Philip presses a short-cut key and they take off, rising slowly from the ground, seeing the hotel grow distant below them, the crickets, the car, the reception, the flashing signs. He turns his finger a quarter circle and they are gazing up into the starry sky. He feels his stomach contract.

"Fantastic," he mumbles.

They fly for awhile in silence. Philip is very concentrated and carefully moves his fingeras though their lives would be at stake if he were to make a wrong move, as though they really could fall straight to the ground and burn up. He lets him work in peace. A little while later a city lights up the sky to the left of them, sending a sickly yellowish glow up toward the stars. "That's Austin," Philip mumbles and adds with a snort, "The world's most creative town."

They are presumably one hundred meters above the town now and his stomach contracts automatically.

"That's the university," he says, pointing to an illuminated area the size of a town, "The largest in North America, sir."

It looks like it is located in the middle of nowhere, like an illuminated figment of the imagination. In its center a tower stretches toward the sky, illuminated in purple. They are too far high to be able to see whether there are any students out. Furthermore, Philip accelerates and they shoot forward at a furious speed.

"There's Crawford," he says, pointing.

"Isn't that where the President lives?"

"The Western White House! It's one of the few places we can't visit. I've tried but it's like flying into an invisible wall. You can see the rest of the town, but there are only 700 inhabitants and it isn't very interesting. There is only one traffic light, but we can actually ignore that."

"Is that Dallas up there?"

"Yup, you can recognize it by the Super Dome, and there's the Museum District. And the monument for the murder of John F. Kennedy and if we make a hard left here we'll soon reach San Antonio, where the Alamo is, if you haven't seen that before?"

"I have, but not like this."

They fly across a dark landscape with low shrubs and fields that have been burnt off but after that follow a wide road where lonely cars with plenty of space between them move through the landscape like tiny fireflies. Philip dives down toward a big truck where a couple of rednecks are sitting on the chassis drinking beer together with some girls they must have picked up somewhere in the wilderness. One of them looks up when he catches sight of them, but it seems something flew in his eye instead which he rubs with his dirty index finger. Philip gives him a knowing glance, smiles confidently, like Tom Cruise before a race in *Days of Thunder*. "Watch as we seriously overhaul them," he says as he speeds off past the truck. He is clearly enjoying it. They arrive in San Antonio shortly afterward.

A Car Without Wheels

With his finger on the iPad he slowly steers them down toward the fortress, past some modern buildings, a hotel next to the square in front of the Alamo and across a wide road. A couple of tourists walk across the square toward Emily Morgans Hotel right across the street, an elderly, Southern looking man who is leaning against a much younger woman. Philip steers them across the fortress, the church, the well, the outer walls that have been shot to pieces.

"Sometimes I pretend it's 1836," he says. "I walk around inside the fortress and can hear the Mexicans outside. It's all very real."

"I can imagine."

"I feel I am there together with Travis and Bowie, I can practically see Bowie sitting in the corner with his knife," he says, smiling a little apologetically. "And Crockett playing the guitar to keep our spirits up."

He doesn't say anything. He has seen the films himself and is impressed by his ability to imagine.

"We're talking about Sam Houston who refrained from rescuing us in order to save up enough energy to beat Santa Anna and the Mexican Army by San Jacinto. Even though it may seem hard to sacrifice your countrymen, it was a smart move."

"Didn't he become president of Texas later?"

"Yes, and he slaughtered the Mexicans while they were having their siesta. I think that says it all. You don't have a siesta when you're in the middle of a war."

"There was actually a Dane who helped defend the fortress," he says, in order to change the topic.

"There were many people who helped defend the fortress."

"He sewed that which would later become the Texan flag. He sewed the Lone Star."

Philip nodded distractedly, yet still steered them away from the fortress, from the square and the two tourists who have just managed to cross the road to the hotel where the man lets go of his young conquest for a short moment in order to hold the door for her. He can't see her face, he would have liked to, but Philip steers them upward, making the couple disintegrate into bricks and treetops.

They continue to fly across San Antonio. There are more people down along the river and you can see dancing silhouettes behind some illuminated window panes. A dog crosses a street but then they ascend once more and the lights disappear below them.

Philip pushes his hand forward with an abrupt movement and the picture flickers before returning as a landscape halfway lost in the darkness. He searches in small circles before finding what he is looking for. The dive down toward a town that chiefly consists of oil pumps and refineries flashing forebodingly in the darkness. Other than that it is completely dark. Philip flies across the town at a low height. This is Texas, he thinks.

"That's where I grew up," he says. "There, to be more precise." He points at a wooden hut that sits right next to an oil drilling site adjoining a fenced in refinery. Garbage is covering the entire front yard and a car without wheels is blocking the entrance. The dry grass is tall and manages to cover the garbage halfway.

"Where does your family live now?" he asks.

"They still live there. Like I said, my dad left the family many years ago to become a professor at a university. The following week my mother managed to find a new man, a retired school teacher who I don't get along with very well. Matthew's his name. My mom can't be alone and even though we never talk about it, my dad's leaving us was hard on her, too."

"It must have been."

"She's a very private person, so she doesn't show her feelings so much. Now she's living at home with Matthew and my two brothers live a couple of meters further down the road."

He pauses for awhile as they float in the air above the house.

"One of my brothers owns the biggest company in town, the weapons company downtown. He makes a lot of money. But he's not exactly a hero. He's never been outside the state, but, then again, many people around here haven't either. Their knowledge of the world is limited to talk shows and neighbors' gossip.

"Do you sometimes see them?"

"Never," he says, hard. "I only see my father."

He's a little quiet before continuing. "My father is very well read. I mostly remember him sitting with a book in his hands. And I'm even named after one of his favorite authors at that time, Philip K. Dick."

"Well, that's not so bad."

"I've actually never read him, I've only seen the

movie adaptations of his books. My dad lost interest in Dick when he seriously began to get popular, that's the way he was, and then I lost interest in reading him. His concept of reality is too fluid for me, anyway, I think."

"Yeah, he's rather indefinable."

Philip looks at him in silence before continuing.

"We weren't allowed to disturb him when he was studying. My mother tried to keep us away from his office if we got too close, slam the door in our faces so that we couldn't help but become more curious. Sometimes he wanted to tell me about what he had read, about literary theory and the Holocaust and then he'd test me on it afterward.If I couldn't remember the answers he'd quickly lose interest." He looks ahead and forgets all about navigating.

"He knew a lot of foreign words and he treated everyone the same. He used as many foreign words with me as he did with his colleagues.

"He sounds like a somewhat strict father."

"He was in a way, too, but in a lot of other ways he was very affectionate and he was also very inspiring. You've got to set the bar high. That's what I learned from him. And everything that I do now, I do it for him." .

While he is talking, he distractedly lets them buzz

back and forth in the air above the city. It looks like a pigsty, it becomes clear, as they fly above it on their way back. Oil leakages must be a daily occurrence and he wonders about the state of health of the residents. "That's where my brother's weapon shop is," says Philip, pointing down at a building that looks like a prison. Ken's Guns, it says.

They make their way back in silence. Perhaps Philip feels that he has said what he wants to say. Or else the sense of nostalgia has rendered him speechless. After a couple of minutes he slows down and heads toward the ground. He can discern a tiny corner of the approaching morning toward the east.

"Thanks for the ride," he says as he pretends to be rubbing some warmth back into his frozen limbs. "That was really interesting, but I think I'd better get back to the motel."

Philip smiles. A new smile. His face muscles at least force the corners of his mouth into a crescent shape. His eyes are cold.

"We just need to try one more thing."

Unacceptable Speech

"It's crazy how much material's been archived," he says, suddenly walking over to the wall with the yellowish filing cabinets. "There are revelations here of every kind: articles, print outs of tape recordings, offensive pictures. A lot of cut out material. Much of it deals with Germans who settled here in Texas in the 40's and 50's.

"Walther Haller," he says, pulling out a folder from the file cabinet, "is now known as Walther Hall and lives in New Braunsfeld. He was first lieutenant in the German army and so on. It probably isn't considered all too relevant today. Furthermore, they all speak very nicely, and that's mostly what I've been looking into so I don't understand why anyone's bothered to record them. I've done some random tests, recorded their language usage, but there was nothing of interest—aside from some residual German in their American pronunciation. I've got it on tape if you're interested."

"Not necessarily."

"But even though I can't use the recordings for anything, I've got access to an amazing collection and listening equipment I can use in my work."

"As a super hero," he adds ironically, but it doesn't register.

"Let me show you how it works," he continues unconcernedly. "I know how to do this. This is what I spend most of my time doing." He turns on another computer standing on a table to the right of the file cabinets. "Himmelstrup, right? Your name is Kristian Himmelstrup?"

He looks at him in awe.

"Relax, I saw it when you booked the rooms and I've manage to develop a practically photographic memory with time."

He tries to think back for a moment. Philip lying with his head on the cartoon, the doorbell that is ringing and Angelina who is reserving two rooms.

"I never gave you my name."

"Of course you did. How else could I know it?"

The computer makes a sound behind him and he turns around toward it with a nervous movement. "Well, let's see, H-I-M-M-E-L-S-T-R-U-P, right?" He turns his face quizzically toward him. "Is that correct?"

He nods.

Philip presses "enter" and turns around toward him.

"It'll just take a few minutes. There are many sources that have to be checked. But I've only asked it to make a search for the last 48 hours, which ought to shorten the time it takes for it to do the search." He can see rows of data rolling across the screen at a raging speed, small letters and lines of codes on a dark blue background. After a short while they stop and about four or five underlined lines stand still, flashing ominously against the dark background.

"There. It found something. It's pretty awesome. It can even sort things out on its own so it can isolate the cuts containing impermissible remarks. But that part of the program isn't quite done yet, so there might be a few slip-ups."

He clicks on the first link and he appears on the screen in what is a somewhat grainy picture quality. He is standing in the line at the airport. The camera must be situated to the right of him on the wall. He can see his lips moving and Philip turns up the volume. "You can filter your way to most everything but I'm pretty certain you're saying 'Fuck' right there." He nods absent-mindedly. Philip finds the next link and now he is at the cash register where he is trying to ingratiate himself and manages to get the man to switch him before the superior interferes. When he is later directed to the other line one can easily hear several utterances of discount in both Danish and American without having to filter it. "You are really giving a bad example, there. And as a visitor to this country you really ought to behave better. Look," he says, pointing at the screen "there are children present."

"They can't possibly hear what I'm saying."

"I can hear what you're saying so I'm sure they can, too."

He doesn't like the direction that this visit is taking.

The last two shots are from the supermarket. One sees him standing at the cash register mumbling a couple of swear words when he is asked to pay and a little while later one sees the shopping cart running into the truck in the parking lot and after that their car disappears into the horizon. "You're saying something unsuitable again," says Philip, squinting his eyes. As if his behavior is no problem, but one inappropriate "fuck" could destroy the world. He rewinds the film and puts it on slow motion. "Fuck, this shithole of a country," and he rewinds it again and turns up the volume. "Fuck, this shithole of a country," he screams. "Fuck, this shithole of a country," Philip repeats automatically. He opens the armrest on the armchair which apparently contains a small compartment for bags of chips and pretzels.

"But enough is enough," he says. "It's people like you that ruin this generous country." He pulls out a small mechanical device and holds it up in front of him, presses a button underneath it and extends it toward him. He discovers too late that it's one of those tasers young girls carry in their purses when they go to parties, and he collapses on the floor from electro shock.

"Yes, well, I'm sorry," he hears somewhere in the distance, "but I had no choice but to punish you for that. I can't just abandon all my principles just because I've gotten to know you a little." He mumbles a few more things which he isn't quite able to register, as he grabs hold of him by the collar andstarts dragging his lifeless body across the floor. Then he loses consciousness. Angelina is the last thing he things about. Maybe he also says her name out loud. At any rate, he can see her bottom dancing before him.

When he gains consciousness, it is dark. Pitch dark. He is lying on a stone floor but when he tries to push himself up from it to a sitting position he discovers that he can't move. He senses something fastened around his wrists and ankles so he assumes he has been tied up. And Philip has been very diligent in doing so. He literally can't move and when he tries to shout for him he discovers that he has also been gagged.

He lies like that for a long time. He can hear some water dripping far in the distance and the sound of small pitter patter sound of little feet close to my head, his head, I'm thinking.

Then the bell rings and class begins.

2

"Puggie died! That's the second part."
from "Heartache" by Hans Christian Andersen
(translated by Jean Hersholt)

The analysis of correspondences represents these deviations visually in factorial planes which weigh them according to distance from χ^2 (chi-square).
from *Homo Academicus* by Pierre Bourdieu

My Best Friend

My best friend looks like a walrus and smells of stinky socks. In the morning he tells in a loud whisper of his nightly escapades as our colleagues walk pastand pretend to be momentarily deaf. He is gay and they can't relate to anal sex with three Mexicans in a parking lot in the east of town or try to understand why he sticks his penis into a hole in the wall hoping someone will take the bait.

He comes from Holland where there are proper saunas. Not like in this Nazi-state, he snorts out loud, making a slender Swedish colleague jump to the side in surprise. She rushes along the hallway and makes a turn at the corner, past the small sofa which is used as an extra office by an American professor because he can no longer be in his own due to the many piles of books that have toppled over. They exchange a knowing glance.

A Peculiar Organism

The university is a peculiar organism. A place where you influence the students to think as society wants them to think. Whether it's free, patriotic conservative, or Lutheran-Evangelical. Free. As though. Free thought is a slogan invented by a prison guard in hell.

You see the young people with their tanned legs in short shorts, soft breasts underneath mini tops, firm buttocks imprinted with the university logo.

No, not now.

You see the young people with their optimistic gaze being blinded by the rigid halogen spot of doctrine (there are a few instances where their eyes light up and the doctrine settles like a pale ring around their iris shining of madness—a thin and fanatic gaze from a higher truth). Their gait grows heavier with the years. The first year they come readily with fresh arguments and stupid comments, but gradually as the yoke of doctrine is placed on their shoulders their answers grow longer and their rebellion has been thought through to death. They can no longer do anything without considering the pros and cons first and they reflect their spontaneity to pieces.

Tradition lays down the rules, they think, or they don't think, you can't get off free once it's been learned by heart. That is the first complication of academia: heavy minds in self-reflection. Joy, let me see, they think, it has something to do with fulfilling one's needs and doing good. Or has it? Because every question has a proper answer that the professor possesses. Especially in the US where the professor is the only one who decides students' grades and a censor is something that cuts out the f-word from the airwaves. As an American student you are at the mercy of one man and woe to the one who thinks independently during the exam. Or the one who has had a disagreement with the professor during the year. On the other hand, social skills are rewarded: good boobs and firm buttocks, subservient submissiveness and trained charm.

You would think the world's greatest minds were convened at the universities to pour forth their knowledge all across the world. You would think it would be the most inspiring environment in which to work. You would think the employees would meet up during coffee breaks to discuss literature, politics, the state of society, films and to share the latest discoveries made within their area of research. You would think that the moon was a one-eyed devil with Satyr legs and angel wings.

It ought to come as a great surprise to everyone just how narrow-minded the discussions that take place at a university in fact are. One thing is that the colleagues in most cases are socially incompetent, that they are too specialized within their area of research to be able to partake in a conversation about ordinary topics, that they don't have time to keep up with the developments in society because they are too preoccupied with morphological developments among not yet discovered tribes in South East Asia. Another thing is that their sense of curiosity has disappeared long ago in standardized preparations for exams and bureaucratic project descriptions. And in addition to that, one is worried one's ignorance outside one's field of study will be revealed. Because it's a matter of being clever about everything other than the outside world. Which is why one displays one's own knowledge as a smoke screen. One doesn't want to pass it on because then it will no longer be an efficient weapon to be used to demonstrate one's opponent's ignorance and thereby dismantle his knowledge. It is all about getting out there, determine the discourse, but at the same time one has to guard one's research results with one's life because they will ultimately decide one's capacity for survival in the academic environment.

In that game, it's a matter of having something on one another that can be used against them later, of undermining the others' position in that environment, making the right alliances and grabbing possibilities that arise on the path to becoming a full professor. Regardless what the price may be. Human relation never pay off. It is a dangerous dead end. Human relations is something you mimic as you consider the ways in which you can abuse your naive interlocutor who hasn't yet understood the rules of the game. Do you stick your penis in the hole hoping someone will take the bait? Really?

Many are willing to commit murder to advance their own career. Or to get one of the coveted offices with triple casement windows and a view across the lawn with the blossoming acacia trees.

CONTINUITY

But the university is also fantastic, I realize I am contradicting myself. Furthermore, I myself am a part of it, as much as I'd like to stand on the sideline and observe the others.

The university passes down experience and ensures society a sense of continuity. The professors are mere marionettes in a millennia old game, wise marionettes who hardly sense the hand on their backs and therefore enjoy their position in society, at best their new Lexus and young lover.

They have placed their wooden heads at the service of tradition, and are now spitting it out to the next generation of possible educators in a closed system of lofty knowledge. The movement makes water spouts in nature, but here it creates pupated larvae that lie with broken wings and mad eyes in the cocoon and never hatch. Continuity. Without it, society would not be a society, and without Ovid, Dante and Hemingway we would be reduced to amoebas. That's the amazing thing, and I was about to forget it again.

Well-Groomed Nails

The tradition takes place in a huge area, in tall houses built in the style of historicism. Right now it's quiet, but during the day the area is bustling with over 50,000 students crossing the streets between classes. It's hot. Weather forecasts are excruciatingly monotonous, and the sun is baking down from a cloudless sky. Right now, it's quiet, except for my steps echoing against the wall next to the sports center, where the lights are just now being turned off. It's midnight, and the bell of the university tower strikes twelve. From there, the first university killer shot and killed 14 people in 1966, starting a new trend in academia. He shot his mother and wife first, then climbed the tower, heavily armed: "I don't understand myself these days," he wrote in his farewell letter. "I should be an average, sensible and intelligent young man. But lately (I can't remember when it started), I've been the victim of a lot of strange and irrational thoughts." To this day, it is difficult to walk past the tower without fearing a killer bullet from the cloudless sky. The university is built up of small knowledge cubicles, where learning flows from the oracle at the pulpit, into space and down the walls, thousands of synchronous stories on all sorts of topics. Walking down the corridors of one of the central buildings, you can hear fragments of the lectures: a little Shakespeare here, photosynthesis there and the masters of silent films in a darkened room rehearsal across form the stairway. Some students are hanging over the banister, but that's not where I am now, I walk past the tower outside, and it's midnight. I squint up at the clock and think of the tower gunman in 1966. I continue through the campus and down into the city, past Capitol and down Congress, to the river. It smells like piss and there nobody in sight. Some bats dive down towards me by the river, and a student throws up over the edge of the bridge. A taxi passes by quietly. Some distance away, my colleague, who looks like a walrus, is having sex with three Mexicans in a parking lot, while the secretary of the Department, who lives just across the river, has just sat down on her soft plush couch to watch a rerun of "Desperate Housewives" for the third time. She looks at her nails and sighs.

Doll Face

The secretary's name is Emily and she is half Mexican. She is the first person you see when you visit the Department. She is one and a half meters tall and sits and talks on the phone and paints her fingernails most of the day. She holds the receiver against her ear with her right shoulder so that she can concentrate on applying nail polish with both her hands free. It can't be ergonomically healthy, she should get a headset. Her smile is very American. When one has been standing in front of the desk with an urgent matter for a while, she puts the nail polish down on the table, places the receiver next to it and smiles: "May I help you?" She says it in a tone of voice that gives you the distinct feeling that you are disturbing her. She has a cute little doll face, and she is enthroned as a little beauty queen, a porcelain figure upon the Department's mantelpiece. She has lived in the United States for so long that she knows the system better than most Americans. She knows, for example, that you don't have to treat visiting instructors with the same respect as the tenured professors ...

They are pleased with her. I know that my neighbor, who works with the Holocaust, kissed her at a barbecue at the start of the semester. Sometimes she also reads women's magazines. The secretary is the most important person in the Department. It is imperative to stay on good terms with her. Otherwise, she may forget to forward your applications or to inform you about approaching deadlines and when there will be free cake. My Dutch friend has not understood. He's furious every time he's stopped by the front office and sees her talking on the phone and polishing her nails. That would not have happened at a Dutch university. "She's incompetent," he hisses, and her sweet face and soft breasts leave him completely cold. Recently, he went to the Head of the Department to complain about Emily, while she herself sat outside the open door and could hear everything. The cow had forgotten to pass on his invitation, to book hotel rooms for his guests, to order food for the reception. Tact is not his greatest forté. Neither is strategic thinking, for that matter ... You have to be on friendly terms with the secretary, I repeat, but Gunther won't listen and will have to make do without getting free cake or receiving Emily's chronic doll smile.

A First Visit

Let's imagine you are going to pay the Department a visit for the first time. You have an errand there. Maybe you want to ask for a semester schedule, maybe you want to hear about the exam requirements for German conversation, maybe you want to invite the secretary out for a cocktail. Maybe you spoke with her at a party of a mutual acquaintance and you have finally mustered up enough courage to go ahead and do it.

No matter what, you first have to cross the lawn with the acacia trees that are possibly in bloom or that are in the midst of dropping their flowers in a delicate, white layer across the grass. You walk up the wide steps and open the double door which makes an audible click, continue across the terra cotta floor to yet another door which you open and go up one flight. You can hear the doors slam shut behind you with their characteristic sound. You imagine that the university may possibly have done research on the sound, like Mercedes researches getting the sound of shutting car doors to signal Mercedes, so that the door slam sounds scholarly, like heavy books and student life all at the same time, slightly intimidating, but also audibly cheerful. At least you are clearly demonstrating you have shut out the outside world.

Anyway, you enter the door of the Department, look around because you enter yet another impersonal hallway and first need to locate the reception. All the doors are identical and the secretary and the Head of the Department aren't more important than the IT employee. You have to spend considerable time looking for all of them.

Perhaps you study the billboards on which the course descriptions are hanging or you look at the board with old pictures of teachers and technical administrative personnel. You can't know that they actually don't look like that at all anymore but have aged unbecomingly by about 20 years each. Then you catch sight of the office over to the right, you walk over and open the door and finally you see, sitting at a big writing desk to the left of the entrance, the secretary polishing her nails while talking on the telephone. You wait politely until she is done before announcing what your errand is. As you wait you listen in on a subdued conversation in the Head of the Department's office situated right next to reception. Perhaps I come out. Perhaps I have been in there to get a scolding for having locked one of my students inside a dark room. I politely smile to the visitor who is waiting for Emily, nod and go out through the door to my office.

THE DEPARTMENT

The Department isn't big. There are about 20 instructors and instruction is offered in Germanic languages, literature and culture: In other words, WWII and the Holocaust. It is located in a building built in the style of historicism on a square south of the tower. The building also contains Spanish and History. It is three storeys and resembles most of the other buildings on campus that are all attempts at imitating a British college. Each storey is designed as a simple labyrinth in which most of the offices are situated along the outer wall and a few without windows in the middle. You can walk around the small office island in the middle of the building by way of an impersonal hallway, thereby passing all the offices, save three that are closer to the reception down another small hallway. That is where my office is located, and William and Hermann have the other two. The doors are brown with an office number pasted on each one explaining to the newly initiated what building they are in, what floor and in front of what office. Next to it there is usually a title and a name: OLS 2.397, Dr. Ronald Keller. A little further down the hallway hangs the billboard with pictures of the instructors.

There are pictures of 19 instructors, two secretaries and a couple of guidance counselors. Most of them are smiling without looking all too happy. They are trying to hit the right balance between seriousness, being forthcoming, and conveying human kindness. Only a few are actually photogenic: Ronald, whose door we stood in front of just before, is a handsome man, and Dusty is a relatively sexy woman. The rest resemble one's well-meaning but somewhat overweight aunt. A single one stands out, Alison, who looks downright scary with her oversized spectacles, a mustache and an oddly blurry head. Gunther, the Dutch guest professor, resembles a walrus while my picture hasn't been hung up yet. I must have forgotten to hand in a picture and am apparently not important enough to be reminded of that.

GUNTHER

Gunther walks by as I am studying the pictures. He positions himself next to me and joins me in looking at the pictures with feigned interest that is supposed to imitate mine. He caricatures his surroundings and has, like me, difficulty taking the world seriously. Which at times poses problems.

"Some rogue's gallery, wouldn't you say?" he mumbles after we have stood in silence for a little while. "That is quite a scary bunch."

I nod.

"Or are you secretly masturbating over Alison's picture?"

I nod again.

He leans forward and closely examines Alison's picture. "Her mustache is almost nicer than mine. That's pretty impressive," he says, grazing his thumb and index finger across the mustache in each direction. He squints and leans forward once more. "Well, I'll be darned," he says and suddenly seems genuinely interested. He points at a small emblem in the lapel of her purple jacket which I hadn't seen. "It's an algize rune," he says in disbelief. "The rune of life."

"What does it mean?"

"It's a Nazi symbol that Himmler used in the Lebensborn program. What the hell is she wearing that thing for?" He shakes his head.

"Isn't it a Nordic symbol?"

"Course it is, but the Nazis stole all the heathen symbols and used them for their own purposes so they would never be the same again."

I nod. I actually knew that.

"Semiotics, my dear friend," he says in an instructive voice. He likes to be more knowledgeable, but who doesn't? Besides, his knowledge is the only thing he has going for him so let him have his small conquests. He neither jogs nor plays squash so he is eager to show off his knowledge like you would a well-trained upper body or an expensive car.

He pulls at my shoulder. "Aren't you supposed to be teaching now? Aren't you going to harass some more of your students? Lock them up or shout at them?"

"Yeah. Are you going in the same direction?"

OMBUDSMEN

I feel that I ought to do this as a responsible teacher. So I stop Joy after class and tell her that she should write her assignments herself. The last one had been flawless and it should have been incomprehensible. Furthermore, I have spoken with the guy who wrote them for her so I feel like I'm on fairly solid ground. She follows behind me crying, and I say that it's okay, but that for her own sake it would be better if she made the mistakes herself and thereby learned from them. That is how one learns things.

Professor Himmelstrup wrote on my paper that he would prefer I not go to a tutor even though I did well on the assignment. After class as I was walking out of the building (CBA) he came up behind me and said that he would prefer I not go to a tutor. I walked away in the opposite direction so he would not follow me. He scares me.

She comes to most of my office hours and I listen to her read out loud, correct her pronunciation and go through the grammar with her. She is very grateful. I am the best teacher she has ever had, and she has had many. She has attended the University for many years. Her pronunciation is atrocious and the only way I can understand what she is saying is by reading the original manuscript."That's fine," I say, "Now it sounds a lot better."

At the end of class he dismissed the class except for me and asked that I stay after in front of the other students. As soon as the other students left, Dr. Himmelstrup started chastising me in a loud voice. After 5 minutes I told him I had to go and apologized that he felt that way. He followed me out of class still chastising me. He said again he wouldn't forget that I went behind his back to the chairperson. I asked him what he meant by that. He said: "You'll see."

Every Friday we watch a Danish TV series. We watch *Nikolaj og Julie*, *Riget* and even *Matador*. When Denmark isn't surrounding you, you'll have to make use of the options at your disposal to create a surrogate Denmark. It quickly turns into a bunch of clichés. Crown Prince

Frederik's marriage, Matador and Dannebrog, but the students enjoy it. Sometimes I think about what kind of images they have created in their minds and how I'm going to alter them with the next piece of information I'm about to give them. It's rather fascinating. "Are there any black people living in Denmark?" or "Are you all communists, or, are there also other parties?" I serve coffee during the Friday film and conclude ten minutes earlier so we can get a chance to discuss it.

Friday, after watching the Danish series *Matador*, I started cleaning up the room (coffee cups etc.), the professor had asked for someone to do so. Yet, while I was finishing in the back of the room he turned out the lights and closed the door intentionally, intentionally creating a dangerous and scary situation for me to find my way out. He's really creating a hostile environment that is not conductive to a healthy learning environment for me.

There are Danish classes every morning. It's an intense program and sometimes it can be difficult to come up with a little variation. There are many ways to acquire a language, and different students learn differently. Some need a grammatical overview before they are able to build further on what they already know, others learn it by speaking. A few times I invite Danes to come visit the class so the students can listen to others besides me speak. At this point they've come to know what I am likely to say and what my dialect is so it's good for them to hear other ways of expressing oneself. The visitors tell about themselves, about Denmark and why they've moved to Texas. It usually has something to do with having more possibilities, lower taxes and bigger personal freedom. Sometimes on account of an American sweetheart. I give them a bottle of wine for their trouble.

Thursday, 2 additional people (non-student friends of his) were in class. They were told by the other students in class that Professor Himmelstrup would let them attend without paying. I asked about a question that he had counted wrong on the quiz yesterday and he asked his friends who were laughing at me. Then the professor said, "Forget it, you won't get credit" and started laughing again. The next 25 minutes, the professor ignored me and I left the classroom and went to Dr. Kennedy's office.

It's a cozy class. There are only seven students which is a vulnerable number but they attend and are determined to contribute and learn something. Even though I don't always have the same motivation for it everyday, I usually walk out of there in a good mood. We have started to be able to have conversations together in Danish and that is very satisfying. It's wonderful teaching something that can actually be measured. It's hard to know whether Habermas and Bourdieu, which I include in my other classes, are expanding their horizons or altering their personalities in any way. In my Danish classes, I know the Danish words that come out of my students mouths are words that I have actually taught them. It's clear they are having a cozy time. There are several hundred students in their other classes, so this is a kind of break for them. They are seen, it is cozy and there are plenty of opportunities for them to speak. They all express their enthusiasm in the regular evaluations.

Professor Himmelstrup came into class agitated (his face was red), pointed at me and announced to the class that I had a problem and that Tracy (his non-student friend) would not be in class because of me. He kept pointing at me and raising his voice. I asked him politely to please stop, that the classroom was no place for it. He yelled at me that it was indeed the place for it. He seemed out of control. Additionally, that day the Professor started making comments about 'old people' and how they should be laughed at. He seems to have a split-personality; I've never seen a Professor be so vicious intentionally in class.

The sequel is prolonged. It involves ombudsmen, commissions, confidential reports and long meetings. Joy can't be in the same room as me which makes the procedure all the more difficult. Long tunics and endless hallways, bad coffee and humorless representatives. It ends up with the other students getting interviewed and I'm cleared. Elementary, my dear Watson. Joy should not have made up seances with witnesses. She even makes up statements from some of the other students and includes their telephone numbers without having asked their permission. Had she stuck with covert one-to-one meetings or sexual harassment it would have been impossible to prove my innocence. So, now she's learned her lesson.

It's a very bizarre experience being the object of a case like that. At no point do I get a chance to tell my version of the story—or just be informed of what the accusations consist of. All I am told is that Joy has spoken with the Head of the Department but when I talk to her I am the best teacher she has ever had. The same day as when she has spoken with the dean and the Head of the Department, she comes during my office hours with a big smile on her face and some simple questions about grammar.

When the case has been closed, Joy's accusation is delivered to me so I can see what the whole thing was actually about. It is 24 pages including exhibits and 9 of them consist of her version of the truth—or a short story that is slightly too long and whose characters are too flat and protagonists slightly blinkered. I am told that the report is confidential and that I am never to show it to anyone or cite from it.

BLACK HOLES

I take the wretched affair in stride until it's over. But then I sense something has changed. For one thing, it sticks like dog's poo on the grooved soles of my shoes which I keep scraping against all the curbs but to no avail. I keep smelling bad. I can see it in my colleague's eyes. They are kind, in a sort of tolerant way, where I feel I have to be grateful for their kindness. It could just as well have happened to them, they say, while it is clear they know that it absolutely never could.

There must be at least one grain of truth in the accusations.

I sense I am growing increasingly suspicious of my surroundings. Not outright paranoid, but I keep my students at an extra arm's length. We no longer meet after class for extra Danish and I no longer serve coffee during the film on Fridays. And I don't compliment them on their new hairdos and avoid cozy small talk with them.

I dream about Joy several times. She is climbing up a drain pipe to my balcony with a knife in her mouth. It's raining and she is soaking wet. When she gets up on the balcony she throws the knife back and forth between her hands before hurling herself at me while holding it in her right hand. She is strong and we fight for a long time. Several times I think I have choked her but she refuses to die, she lies still on the balcony only to suddenly, on impulse, start dashing at me again.

There are a couple of times when I also experience falling into a black hole, where I sit in the office breaking into a cold sweat and getting a stomach ache before going to class. And thinking everyone wishes the worst of me. That it is a conspiracy. That the students, the Department, the University, have ganged up on me to break me. In order to frame me for something I possibly didn't do.

The Paranoid System

Despite my feelings of paranoia and depression I go through with teaching the class. It's not so bad, after all. That's how it is to become a grown-up and encounter your first psychopath. Your innocence disappears and your sense of fear starts to settle in.

Aside from that it doesn't help there is a clear parallel to the justice system in a society that surrounds me during a war on terror, where one is guilty without the possibilty to appeal or defense.

A couple of times I am stopped outside the secure walls of the university and asked to show my passport. "They follow you if they detect an accent," an officer confides to me, "and they have undercover officers on the streets in town." According to the Patriot Act, all foreigners must carry passports on their person at all times if they don't want to risk imprisonment or getting downright deported. The terrorists who flew into The World Trade Center didn't have their papers in order, either, the officer tells me.

His name is Henry and he teaches in the military building. I meet him in line at the post office and we strike up a conversation. There aren't all that many of us in line but the post lady is taking her sweet time, disappearing out back for about a quarter of an hour, chit-chatting with the Mexican cleaning assistant who is washing the floors behind her.

The university is its own little mini community, a mini cosmos with its own rules and mores. With its own zip code and police force, shops and hotels, cinema and pool hall.

Things that aren't ascribed much value outside, mean everything in here, and everyone is spun into invisible threads that create the ivory tower's slight skeleton. This is where you can score by way of your position, while you wouldn't stand a chance outside, as Henry says just before approaching the counter. "Outside, the girls only care about how much you earn." But in here that's not the way the cookie crumbles.

New Prose

Sometimes I introduce my students to the latest Danish prose. I don't want to cheat them out of that. I recite something to them and then explain it so they'll know what to say at the exam or what to write in their essays

There is a plant standing in the window sill. It is a geranium.

"Look, a geranium," says Herbert.

"Yes, I say.

"It reminds me of my uncle Otto. He also had a geranium."

"I think it's a rather common plant," I say.

"Yes," says Herbert.

"It looks like the Michelin Man dressed in a tutu," I suggest and Herbert smiles.

"That's Metilla Jakobsen," I say and write her name on the board, along with her birthdate and her most significant works. "She attended the Writer's School. She writes in a very fine minimalist style, but with a lot of humor. A dry, shaven down sort of humor. She really understands how to sense a scene, to take in the small peculiarities of reality. Notice the thoughts the geranium triggers and how the smile is ambiguous. It's impossible to say what Herbert is, in reality, smiling about. And reality is truly a central word here," I say while thinking about having sex with the little Korean in the back row. A girdle and a patent bra are involved across the writing desk from behind, but then the fantasy starts to flicker and the image disappears and I am back standing in front of the classroom holding Matilla Jakobsen in my hand and a piece of chalk and sensing the beginning of an erection.

THE CUTEST BREASTS

I actually haven't noticed her at all in the classroom. She is Korean but she never says anything and sits hiding in back of the classroom next to one of the permanent desks. She isn't someone you'd normally notice, a little coy, small and shy.

She wants to talk about the last essay she wrote in which she was given a compassionate C. She looks up at me and smiles awkwardly. Then she takes off her jacket. I explain a little about maintaining the silver thread and formulating problems, then she takes off her sweatshirt. There are also too many spelling and grammar mistakes, I say, as she tosses the t-shirt. Perhaps she could get someone to read it through before handing it in?

She is wearing a small negligee and I hold back on the criticism. She has the cutest little breasts and I can look right through to them. She isn't wearing a bra and she bends over the table toward me. They look soft. I am almost certain they would feel like Angelina's buttocks. I decide to ignore the fact that she is sitting half-naked in front of me and now it's too late to mention it and tell her to put her clothes back on.

"What can I do to get a better grade?" she asks. "I am willing to do anything." My thoughts have already jumped across the table and pulled off the last morsel of clothing she is wearing, something which they would do many times the next couple of days. I myself remain sitting. Well, you don't have that far to go, I say. Whereupon she puts her clothes back on, piece by piece and quickly leaves, while I remain sitting and feeling older than ever before.

Ronald, a colleague soon ready for retirement who is in the midst of writing a novel about his own death, trumps my story. We are sitting in front of the hearth in the Faculty Club with a drink and our legs discreetly crossed. He is wearing a red pullover and looks like a man of the world. "There was a naked student on my desk," he says, stirring the ice cubes in his drink. "She wanted to talk about her grades. When I went to the computer room to get a copy of her status she took off all her clothes and jumped onto the table." We don't know whether the idea emerged spontaneously, but the result is the same: a naked student on one's writing desk. He empties his glass and smiles at the recollection. "When

I saw her, I said, 'I'm going to leave this room while you put your clothes back on,'" but who knows what actually happened.

I'm trying to imagine what it must feel like. Standing naked in your professor's office putting your clothes back on. Does she think about shooting herself, or is she already considering her next move as she pulls her panties over her tanned thighs? Does she still enjoy the tension and the touch of pain? And does she know whether the mission has been successful? That the image of her naked body has been implanted into Ronald's brain who will think of her positively when the grades have to be given out in a few weeks? That it is almost guaranteed he'll give her a higher grade in order to demonstrate that he didn't take offense? And in order to avoid being accused of sexual harassment?

NAPOLEON

It's at the end of the semester they start taking their clothes off. With a couple of weeks to go, the chemistry between the teacher and the students changes significantly. Of course, not everyone shows up to strip down, but most show up to make their existence known. So you can remember their face when it comes to grades. They are very skilled. They make it seem like the most natural thing in the world is for them to show up and elegantly weave in how much your classes have meant to them, how hard they have worked and how they will use what they have learned in their future studies, work life, well, just life in general. They hadn't realized how great a writer Hans Christian Andersen actually was, how much wisdom could be gleaned from him.

There is no external examiner, so the teacher decides everything, from how the course is structured to the grading. Students are given a grade calculation when the semester starts to which they pay close attention: This percentage of the grade for class attendance, this much for class participation, and this much is given for quizzes and assignments. You can decide in advance how active you want your students to be by prioritizing active participation highly. Or not. Under no circumstances will you get critical questions. At first, I read the criticism into their questions myself, interpreting their banality as a form of advanced irony. But from the puzzled look on their faces when I, in turn, responded to them with sarcasm, I realized they had meant them quite literally.

The grading itself entails applying percentage calculation on a rather advanced level, which makes me break into a cold sweat. But the students have carefully calculated the whole thing, and they tell me that at this point in time they have 88.97% and ask what they can do to earn the last remaining percentage. As mentioned, they are willing to do anything, they say, while I try to keep my fingers to myself, sticking them into the lapel of my uniform jacket.

A Tiny Squeak

Alison allegedly reported a colleague for sexual harassment at one point, and it's a constant joke between Gunther and I. Alison looks like a colorful mole in her purple velour dress. She has several patchwork dresses in cobalt blue and brown. I don't know if she sews them herself.

Her glasses are so scratched it's a wonder she can see out of them, but she navigates the corridors with ease as she moves from one colleague to the next in order to stir up intrigue. Maybe she just knows the labyrinth of the hallways so well she is able to navigate without having to use her vision, or maybe she sees better than we think. She keeps pushing her glasses further up her nose with the back of her hand, as if that might help, and has a habit of pulling her upper lip up a little as she does so. Sometimes she also makes a tiny squeak during department meetings, either when she loses her focus or is about to fall asleep. Then a little squeak can be heard, which is actually rather charming, it only becomes embarrassing when she looks around and pretends as if it's nothing.

The colleague was later fired. I don't think there was a connection with the sexual harassment case, but what do I know? Gunther has tried asking around, but hasn't been able to discover anything. All compound phrases containing the word "sex" are of great interest to him. One of the older professors, Sigrun, told him that the colleague had been genuinely interested in Alison, but had accidentally declared it rather awkwardly at a symposium dealing with gender roles during the Second World War. We think Alison should be flattered by any interest given to her as a woman, but her true passion is and will always be Hitler. It's going to take a lot more than a romantic scholar to change that.

HITLER

Most everything at the Department is about World War II: Hitler, Jews, and the Holocaust. Often when you walk into a classroom, the previous instructor will have forgotten to wipe the blackboard clean, and you can be sure there will be something about Eva Braun, Leni Riefenstahl or the Holocaust. Not to mention the titles of macabre books I've never heard of, important dates in the 40's and fascist slogans in quotation marks. I get the feeling they intentionally leave them on the blackboard as a reminder to the rest of us. You don't erase Riefenstahl just like that, and we mustn't forget the Holocaust. When we discuss possible guest lecturers at teacher meetings, it is essential that they have written a really good book on Jewish persecution or made important discoveries in regard to post-fascist imperialism. New German Literature is from 1950 and always deals with the post-war period, and should a current German movie find its way into the library, it's sure to be in black and white and about Hitler's final days, with bombings aplenty accompanied by orchestral music.

Most of my colleagues speak German to me, and even though I struggle with tenses and endings, it hasn't yet dawned on them that the northern German province of Denmark has its own language, which may be Germanic, but is neverthless significantly different from "real German." They attribute my comprehension problems to dialectal differences, and I just raise my hand tentatively in greeting: Sieg!

THE DREAM

I have a recurring dream in which I am working late. I can hear the other teachers leaving their offices and locking their doors. Then, the sound of their reverberating footsteps in the half-empty building, and the large doors to the stairway slamming heavily behind them. Outside, darkness falls. I can't see it, though, because I don't have access to any windows. My office faces inwards, and there are no windows in the common areas either. But I can sense it, there's something in the air that gives it away. It's dark outside, everyone has gone home and I'm alone with my computer. The fluorescent tube in the ceiling blinks reassuringly down at me.

I get up and walk down the stairs to the ground floor to get a Coke from the vending machine. I greet a cleaning lady on the first floor who mumbles a greeting back. She's here illegally and doesn't understand a word of English, so I just smile and walk past her down the hallway to the vending machines. It takes a while to get the Coke machine to accept my one-dollar bill, which keeps crumpling in the cash slot and being spat out with an annoying buzz.

As I turn around with my Coke in my hand, I see a door I hadn't noticed before. It's standing ajar. I can see a staircase leading down into the darkness to what must be a basement. I had no idea the building had a basement, but at the same time, I'm not so surprised. It's not something I've given much thought, and, anyway, why wouldn't they include a basement while they were at it? I walk to the door, open it fully and look down the stairs.

There's something about the staircase that's enticing. A soft light spreads up from below, and it all seems unusually cozy. So I step through the door and walk down towards the light.

I enter a large room with a stone floor and high ceilings. In the center of the room is a throne situated on a raised platform. There is a man sitting on the throne and as I get closer, I can see that it is Hitler. He's easy to recognize with his square mustache and combed over hair. He looks at me mildly. Then he asks for a sip of my Coke. Without opening his mouth. I hesitantly hand it to him. He takes a sip and then wipes his mouth with the edge of his sleeve. Behind him is a blackboard with his biographical data and the most important battles of the Second World War. A row of chairs are set up in front of it, and over in the corner is a sand table with little tin soldiers and model cars. Then Hitler burps loudly and I look up.

Then the whole thing isn't so impressive after all. Suddenly, history turns into mere memory, and all the accumulated knowledge that is left on the blackboards after class is over is more a tribute to the old man in the basement than to the rest of us.

But what is memory in contrast to source criticism and historical perspective?

Whenever teachers are in doubt, they go to the basement. Hitler will willingly answer everything. Sometimes he conducts study groups on specific topics, I learn in a later dream. This explains the division of the Department. It is not only divided into A, C and F parking spaces, offices with and without windows, employees with and without PhDs, it's also divided according to who has access to the source in the basement. I don't know how one is admitted into the inner circle, but I can see who is there and in the following weeks I observe their hidden greetings and knowing smiles. I can't find a pattern in the greetings, but my suspicions are confirmed when I find some paper in the photocopier with a swastika pre-printed on the letterhead. I have to make an invitation to a movie screening at the Danish club and am a bit surprised when it is printed out on Hitler's letterhead. I tell Gunther when we have a cup of coffee with some colleagues later in the day, but he brushes it off as a joke. He's not surprised, he says.

American Ignorance

Gunther often wonders out loud about their stupidity: the students, his colleagues, the American nation. He tells anecdotes about how stupid the students are in class and plays the various roles with a caricature voice. In a sneering tone, he reproduces their hopeless pronunciation of Derrida and Foucault, with their American "r's" and their tendency to put the emphasis on all the wrong syllables. He trashes most of them, but, then, he isn't exactly endowed with a cheerful spirit. Most of the comparisons he makes are in Holland's favor: the saunas are better, the food, the toilet paper, the students.

He's just joined Weight Watchers and soon he won't look like a walrus anymore. More like a large seal. He talks with enthusiasm about the rituals and the fine silver and bronze stars he has already garnered. There's something about weighing yourself in front of others, the collective applause and the gold stars when you've earned them, the silence when you haven't. You don't celebrate losers. You don't even comfort them in any meaningful way.

We drive around the area together, the seal and I, exploring the bush, abandoned oil fields, snakes and rocks. A few times I also accompany him on research trips to German villages with shops full of Tyrolean music, garden gnomes and sauerkraut. Aside from that, we meet in each other's offices or have lunch together at the café next to the Department. Healthy salads with two bags of Newman's dressing and croutons. Occasionally, we are also invited to the homes of some of the others from the Department, or we lure some of them to a café.

Gunther is very active, running around all over Texas, and never missing an opportunity to do fieldwork. He interviews cowboys, takes notes from his sauna visits and runs his thick head against every American wall he can spot. He ignores even the most obvious cultural codes, stays too late at parties, talks too loud and long at meetings and has yet to shed his Dutch sense of humor. He laughs at the wrong things and tries to smooth out a tense situation by making politically incorrect comments. Preferably, he talks about sex.

We are both aliens in transit and we are treated as such. The advantage to this is that we are seen as impartial, and in a way, we are. We don't know the whole story, but must piece together our own narrative based on all the gossip we hear in the hallways, offices, receptions and cafés.

On a good day, you can go from one office to the next, taking turns slandering your colleagues until you've reached the end of the row. The revelations are usually whispered to you as if you're the only person in the world who is allowed to know. You're not, and it's not exactly confidential information. The slander is part of a larger strategy in which everyone takes part, so that eventually everyone is spun into each other's web. Just knowing the secrets means you are enmeshed. Like a fly is enmeshed in a spider's web.

"Paulina's not very competent," Alison says confidentially, "but she's been kissing up to the right people and it's paying off."

"Alison has hardly published anything," says Paulina. "But she's as scheming as they come, and it pays off. She's brilliant at playing people off against each other. You have to watch out for her."

"Alison and Paulina have teamed up against

Hermann," says William. "They don't like it when men upset their apple cart."

"Jenny is not up to the job at all," says Tim, but according to Hermann, he would like to replace her as Head of the Department, so he isn't to be trusted. "Ronald was hired without any real qualifications," says Jenny, "but it seems he had somebody under his thumb."

It's rare that Jenny speaks disparagingly about anyone, and she delivers the information without sounding gossipy. As if it were a neutral piece of information. We're sitting in her office after I've finally been cleared of charges for harassing my students. The system has finally gotten around to talking to the parties involved, including myself, whereupon the air just slowly went out of that balloon. Until then it had been inflated to the full, and everyone was pointing at it and showing it to each other, certain of my guilt. Maybe Jenny knows that she didn't handle the case optimally, and now she feels like she owes me something. A little piece of jovial gossip to demonstrate that we have long since moved on from that little affair. Now we're just colleagues again, on equal footing. I may have been at her mercy a few hours ago and had to behave submissively to get her to close the case, but now we're sitting in her, that is, the Head of the Department's, office and having a chat about the other, less fortunate elements of the department: the colleagues.

Jenny is not very tall, and has chestnut brown hair and brown eyes. She looks like someone you immediately want to like. There is something very human about her, something naive and innocent at the same time, and she talks about her children, her husband and her hobbies (movies and whist). As Head of Department, she tries to build good relationships with everyone.

When I first arrived, she immediately told me that her grandfather was half Norwegian: "Hei, hei," she said and smiled.

Her last name is Kennedy, and she discreetly weaves in her heritage when talking to new people. She is distantly related to the Kennedy clan and once had dinner with Ted and his second wife, Victoria. And 200 other guests, Paulina tells us mockingly, one day when we're talking about Jenny.

The Meetings

Jenny Kennedy leads the faculty meetings, but she doesn't dare interrupt the others. She is the youngest of the real professors, and it is the others who made sure she got tenure and later became Head of Department. If she gets off on a tangent about labor-intensive tasks or complex ideas, they look at her with a supervisor's gaze and she quickly forgets all about it. The rest of us don't say much, but look down at the table or doodle on our spiral notebooks, draw patterns in the crumbs from the cookies and drink our filter coffee. Or: I don't drink it. I made it, so I know there was a moldy filter in the machine and saw how the furry mushroom coating had grown all the way into the funnel. I put a new filter on top and almost threw up at the thought of the coffee running through the mold and into the pot. At the same time, I had an inexplicable feeling of joy in my body. They don't usually make coffee at meetings. It's a Danish custom I've introduced. They really appreciate it, smiling as I put the pot on the table.

The head of the Head of the Department signals when she wants to speak and doesn't dare interrupt Alison and Tim. The meetings become very long. The others ignore her when she raises her hand, and she can sit for a long time waving her cheap pen in the air as the adults talk about difficult students or unattainable academic titles, their latest articles in reputable journals. They don't hold back when it comes to their own significance. "My latest article in the Journal of Dutch Gender Studies will probably revolutionize science." Hm hmm, we nod mutely as we run our fingers through the crumbs. A couple of the others sit and look into their coffee cups, turning them around in their hands before getting up to go to the restroom. Ronald smiles at me across the table. I managed to tell him to stay away from the coffee. He opens a Mountain Dew, looking like he'd rather have a whiskey.

RONALD

Ronald has worked at the Department for over 40 years. There is always a Ronald at a Department like this. Someone who has persevered even though he doesn't really fit in. And who can't wait to quit his job. He usually smells a bit like beer. He teaches in crime fiction and has a cane in which he can store 10 centiliters of liquid if he feels like it. He unscrews it one day outside the main building and shows me the glass tube of bourbon. Now we sometimes have a little sip together before we go our separate ways to teach. He has six dogs that he drives around in his old Dodge Ram. I believe his wife died in an accident a number of years ago, but I can't get anyone to tell me the full story. I only get bits and pieces. Maybe he's never been married. Maybe he's really gay. In any case, he invites me for drinks at his regular hang-out, and you can tell that he comes there often because the waiter comes over to sit at our table to small talk with us and it almost seems like he's trying to set us up. Then again, maybe he's just a professional. Or maybe I'm just paranoid.

He takes a picture of us together and Ronald

gets me to tell the waiter about Denmark, to which he listens with great interest. It's one of the most exotic things he's ever heard. "Fantastic," he says and goes to serve a regular customer at the bar. Ronald has the most attractive office in the department, a corner office with three large windows and an impressive view. He says many people don't approve of it and can't wait for him to leave. He plans to write a crime novel in which he himself is murdered and the motive is that someone wants his office. He goes through all the suspects for me on the way to class, all our colleagues and their possible motives. There's also something about Indians in Arizona and a smuggling operation to Mexico. He's researched it all and just needs to write the book.

I think he has slept with one of the other professors back when she was a student at the department. She tells me, not him, but she's not a credible source, so I still haven't ruled out the possibility that he's gay. He was really hot back then, she says. As well as a playboy. He doesn't show up at the Department all too often anymore. He stays at home as much as possible and is waiting for the day when he can start receiving his pension.

Under Suspicion

It could be Tim McMurian who killed Ronald, because he has so many piles in his office that he can hardly get in himself. I've never seen anything like it. There are papers from floor to ceiling, on the desk, on the floor, on the chair just inside the door. A small path has been made leading to the desk and the chair behind it, but it's impossible to see if he's in if you happen to pop by.

If you ask him about something, he always has an article somewhere. Sometimes he finds it and puts it on loan in your pigeonhole for a while afterwards. They tend to be German-language articles, but he also cuts them our from the *The Washington Post* and the Danish newspaper *Politiken*.

It could also be Sigrun, who has been a full professor for as long as Ronald, yet only has two casement windows. She doesn't seem to feel it quite matches her position. She manages a million-dollar fund donated to the Department by a bunch of old Nazis who needed to get rid of their war booty before they died, something I found out only recently. It could be one of the newer ones, but they probably wouldn't be able to get their hands on the office anyway. Jenny, maybe? After all, she is the Head of the Department and will probably have a hard time making do with her small office once she becomes a regular employee again.

Alison, who looks like a mole, is also under suspicion. She wants to be in charge of the department and is in the process of positioning herself as head of department so that she can attain official power. Personally, I think she's the one who killed Ronald, but he adamantly denies it.

MICKEY MOUSE

Alison puts blackmail potential stories on record. She creates them herself. At a cocktail party, she'll back you into a corner, leaving you defenseless with your wine, your nachos and carrot sticks.

She stands in front of you in her big velvet dress, and you know immediately that the battle is lost. She pushes her glasses up on her nose and frowns myopically:

"Mickey Mouse is gay" or "James Bond never eats dessert", she begins, and then explains her observations.

When she's done and you're kind of obliged to contribute something, she asks what you think about the speaker, about Paulina or about Jenny as head of department. She says it in a tone of voice so that there can be no doubt you and she are united in liking them less. She'll write your answer down later in her notebook so she can use it against you when an opportune moment arises. "Ronald is writing a book about the Department," I say, "in which he himself is murdered." It was the best I could come up with, and Alison looks pleased as punch.

You get the sense there's more to her than that. That she's trapped in a role she's playing to the best of her ability. She's clearly one of those people who has struggled at school and is now taking revenge. She collects all the academic degrees and professional recognition she can and uses them as weights in the great scales of existence to counterbalance mockery, humiliation and physical defeats of her past.

She sees the body as an uncomfortable shell whose only justification is that it transports the brain around in a sensible way. She is a feminist. She is reluctant to see women reduced to sex objects and believes there is still a long way to go before gender equality is achieved. In this, she has Paulina's full support, even if her approach is slightly different. On a daily basis, they ignore each other, but they sometimes talk about it at parties when they end up in a corner together at the end of the night.

POETRY BOOK

Paulina looks like a frog. She's small and squatty, but it's not so much that. It's something about her eyes, which are deep in their sockets and can look in all directions at once. And her perpetual smile, a little too wide. She's the kind of person who holds your gaze too long. She says something and then when others would look away, she holds your gaze as if something more is coming. "And then he shot himself just outside Hanover..." It's very uncomfortable.

In her own mind, she is a femme fatale who has to fight men off. For the sake of the challenge, she mostly goes after gay men. She has slept with my predecessor, who was gay. He left all his personal documents and pictures on my computer so it's hard not to take a peek. In one of the pictures, he's all oiled up, shirtless and wearing overalls. He looks good, but it still seems a bit corny. Gunther fears Paulina's advances. She has recently given him her poetry book to write in. "A poetry book," he groans. "What the hell do you write in a poetry book?" I suggest the truth, but he doesn't buy that.

Still, he invites her to a barbecue at his house and she shows up in a tight dress and pink cowboy hat. Later that night, she picks up an old Chinese guy at a gay bar. He's wearing a black cowboy hat, so they have a hard time kissing. He's a few centimeters shorter than her, so their shadows keep bumping into each other. At one point, she pushes hers back around her neck so that it dangles on a string around her neck. They look sort of cute together, in a slightly pitiful way. Later in the evening they go to her house together, but we never find out what they get out of it. The story disappears into a void for lack of an omniscient narrator. Paulina giggles coyly and brushes it off when I ask her the next day.

The Woman With the Dogs

Ronald shakes his head. He walks past us in the hallway outside the office as I ask Paulina about the previous evening. He's not crazy about Gunther and his sexual obsession and probably thinks he's contaminated me. "He's too uninhibited, even for me," he says when I retell some of Gunther's best stories, "but, then, I'm probably a bit old-fashioned." Paulina merely giggles coquettishly before waltzing off to her office.

Apart from Gunther, who doesn't really count because he's my best friend, Ronald is the only other person who shows any interest in my presence in Texas. He takes a picture of me one of the first times I'm in his office. He wants to see if the camera works, he says, he's just changed the battery on it, and I wonder if he's gay after all.

It must have been after the reception for Gunther's visiting lecturer, a feminine professor from Lübeck, who had spoken about gender expression in the Third Reich for almost three hours. There was no end to all of the questions. Afterwards, we gathered in the lobby outside the lunch café for nachos and white wine, where the discussion continued in small groups:

"But think of Juana Bormann, the woman with the dogs, how could he avoid her when he talks about..."

"Maria Mandel."

"Yes, as in Lichtenburg and Mühldorf..."

"Ordered music for the executions."

"Ilse Koch."

"Or Hitler's own phallic handwriting in..." Ronald saved me, that's where I came from. I don't remember what he said, but I do remember floating weightlessly with a glass of white wine between the small study groups when he came over and pulled me out and up to his office, where he took a picture of me with his recharged camera.

Ronald asks about Denmark, the trip to the US, the airport, immigration, what I think about the Department, the country, the war on terror. I quickly realize I can tell him anything. I don't have to filter out all the politically incorrect statements I'd normally say, something which I've already gotten used to having to do. He tells me about his use of weed and alcohol, past relationships with women and questionable academic projects. He has even made out with the department's gray eminence, he laughs. "Sigrun, damn it," he says when I look at him in wonder, "I'm not proud of it, but it's true." He looks into the air and repeats it lower to himself, as if he doesn't quite believe it himself: "I've made out with Sigrun."

A Burrito with Egg Filling

Sigrun used to tend sheep on the moors somewhere in England before moving to the US with her parents. She spent the money to buy her own small flock of sheep that lived in the bike shed. She talks about it at a faculty party after a few drinks. We're at the home of Hitler Mustache and his wife, nervously fidgeting with platters of chips and salsa and little burritos with egg fillings. She talks too loud and too long, but somehow she has created an atmosphere of uninterruptibility. She herself is standing on the moors with flushed cheeks and her skirts fluttering about, her eyes glassy and dreamy, while the rest of the party look down into their empty glasses. I smile at the wife of Hitler Mustache as she passes by with platters and take a burrito with egg filling onto my plate.

Sigrun wears purple socks and speaks in a soft voice. She often sits on the floor when we have meetings, with her legs crossed, and just inside the door. She wears glasses that magnify her pupils, and her large eyes follow the movements of the meeting from a frog's perspective. Sometimes she's stoned and her pupils dilate a few extra millimeters. There are rumors she and Dusty get high together and may have even slept together. The latter is only hinted at. I've never seen the two greet each other in public, but, then, there are many people whom Dusty doesn't greet.

Sigrun's role at the Department is difficult to grasp. She's a kind of gray eminence who, while being stoned, floats high above the waters. She's long since weaned herself off all niceties and quickly comes to the heart of the matter during rare moments of clarity. She can be brilliantly clear-minded and can also be completely absent-minded. Sometimes at teacher meetings you would expect Sigrun to respond, but she'll just sit there with an absent gaze and a quiet smile and be in a completely different place. Other times, she'll fly into a temper without warning and put her colleagues in their place before they've even gotten a chance to defend themselves.

The others are afraid of her and rumors are numerous and are spread in whispers. She has an older friend who occasionally comes to the department, and she is treated with great respect by the older colleagues. Whether it's because she's dating Sigrun, I don't know, but it seems to go deeper than that. Jenny is extraordinarily smarming in her company, so maybe it has something to do with money.

On one occasion, I bump into Sigrun and the older friend when I've been over for my evening workout and come back to the Department to pick up my papers. I expect to find the Department empty and am surprised to hear muffled chatter and laughter down the hallway. I go downstairs and hear it coming from Tim's office. The door is ajar and I see the back of Sigrun and hear the sound of her friend's voice talking to Tim. It's something about World War II again, I hear Buchenwald mentioned, but also something about St. Olaf College and being in bad company. Hitler mustache is mentioned in this context. When I knock on the door, Sigrun quickly turns around and closes the door, her eyes flashing.

THE HITLER-MUSTACHE

The Hitler Mustache is my neighbor. His real name is Hermann. He's Ronald's only friend at the Department, so I sometimes see him when I'm with him. Hermann speaks excellent German. He teaches German pronunciation and conversation, and I can hear him lecturing the students during his office hours: "Buchen-wald," his tone is friendly but stern. His door is open and I can see the students sitting on the edge of the flimsy chair just inside of it, next to the desk, where Hermann is waiting for the right answer. He's not tough on them, but he sets high standards, both for himself and his surroundings, let's put it this way.

He has a mustache that looks like Hitler's and always wears a leather cap and leather vest. You'd think someone would explain to him it's inappropriate, but the transformation has probably happened gradually, so he and those around him haven't noticed the change. Soon I myself will probably start to resemble Queen Margrethe. To soften the Nazi look, he wears a scarf and patterned suspenders, and is a gentleman through and through. The Red Pimpernel meets Captain Jespersen.

He plays tennis and swims once a week at Barton Springs or Hamilton Pool, and when he does he has demonstratively wet hair and a towel over his shoulder when he arrives at eight o'clock.

STRAWBERRY PUNCH

Dusty swims every morning in Barton Springs. I sometimes meet her over there, but we pretend we don't know each other. But then again, who wants to greet coworkers in swimsuits? Who wants to be reminded coworkers have a body?

She is unmarried, but has a boyfriend who is a fisherman. He has a boat in Corpus Christi and is away for months at a time. He's a handsome young man, weathered and muscular with a well-groomed beard and a twinkle in his eye.

I've been to her house a couple of times. One time I dropped a bowl of strawberry punch on the floor, leaving exotic fruits all over the long carpet.

"That's okay", she said, "I wanted a new one anyway."

A little later, I broke the back of her armchair as I leaned back in it holding a bowl of chips. For a while after that, we mostly pretended we don't know each other. She has an indeterminate gaze that seems to be looking right next to you, making you wonder if she's even aware of your presence.

Apart from me, I think she only sees William in private. On the other hand, there are a lot of people she doesn't like. For example, her office is next to Tim McMurian's, but they don't seem to get along. He was part of her hiring committee and she's heard through the grapevine that he tried to block her.

She tells me this one evening when we have dinner at William's house. Her PhD was about the Mosaic religious community, I can't exactly remember what her angle was, but she had forgotten to credit an article that Tim had co-authored, which he was sure she had read and used. "Sheer dishonesty!" he allegedly shouted during a review committee meeting. He was reportedly very upset.

"I hadn't even read it," she says. "It wasn't relevant to my thesis at all." Knowing the story, it's interesting to observe the two of them when they're together. How they avoid each other without showing it too demonstrably, like two plus poles in a magnetic dance. How the words they use to address each other are usually double-edged and designed to upset the other. Or to score cheap points with the initiates.

Reflections

Scholars are looking for themselves everywhere. When a new journal lands on Emily's desk at reception, you take turns flipping through it to see who has managed to contribute an article about your field of research. Are you quoted? Have you been mentioned? Have you been passed over in silence? The worst thing is, of course, if you're not mentioned but one of your colleagues is.

"I know he read my article about the Polish women's work stoppage in 1943," says Paulina. She is frantically flipping through a new magazine about something to do with gender and politics. I can't read the title because her hands are shaking with rage, so the magazine is dancing around in front of her. And I don't dare ask. She has red spots on her neck and her breathing is labored. "I told him about it myself at the Maria Mandel conference last year." She looks appealingly over at William, who is pouring coffee for me. He smiles back.

"What a jerk," he says.

"He's practically stolen all my arguments," she gasps

even though all three of us know that isn't true. Paulina is not a researcher who is often cited, let's put it that way.

A Delicate Glass Eye

William is my office neighbor. He is always good for an American smile and a harmless remark, and he has also once kissed the secretary at a start-of-semester party. Our offices are located a little out of the way in the department, down a small hallway and across from a broom closet and The Hitler Mustache. William lost one of his eyes in a cheap hospital before he got proper insurance. He was scheduled for a simple surgical procedure and it went wrong. He had signed a disclaimer, so he can't even sue them. He has a good glass eye, and I don't actually realize it until he tells me himself. Now I can see it's staring a bit rigidly straight ahead. I choose to focus on the other one when we occasionally talk. It seems more natural.

He also has a little wrinkle in front of each ear. Like there's a little too much facial skin. As if whoever was modeling him was interrupted just before finishing.

William works with the Holocaust, but he is actually a linguist specializing in the German dialects that have survived in Texas. He goes out with his little tape recorder and collects speech samples. He brings a list of words that he tests on the old Germans and tries to get them to speak German. Some of them can only remember a few words, "Guten morgen" or "Haus," and they laugh in a somewhat shy and senile manner when he speaks German to them. "Jah, jah," they say so as not to lose face, and then he doesn't know if they have understood or not. It's that easy to pretend, I think as I listen to the tape recording. It takes very little to keep a conversation going, a few reflex grunts and mechanical utterances, or a single attentive eye searching for my reaction while the other stares rigidly down at the floor as the tape runs out.

William wants me to conduct the same sort of thing in the Danish colony of Danevang in southern Texas. "But they're not Nazis," I try, but he won't hear of it.

He is one of the brightest academic stars in the department, and the only one who has managed to achieve his position purely on the basis of hard work. He knows how to play the game, sure, but he concentrates on doing an excellent job so that there's no way he can be turned down when it comes time to negotiate a raise.

He tries to stay friends with everyone, avoids political commentary—and is impossible to get to know. He has four assistants to collect material for him, graduate students, while he himself works day and night.

Honey and Musk

Dusty is in some ways William's opposite, and then again, not. She's been here as a student and has never fully recovered. She doesn't seem like the sharpest knife in the drawer, either. She may be working on something about Jews, nevertheless her area of research isn't clearly defined and she tends to use common words when she speaks. She smiles awkwardly. She knows it doesn't look good. She teaches Norwegian and speaks it pretty fluently. I make the classic mistake of assuming language and identity go hand in hand. I forget to turn off my autopilot and talk to her like a Scandinavian. She looks a little startled, but I don't take it seriously. I'm so used to thinking of language as indicating one's cultural identity even if it may, at times, contain deviations, because in the end it still indicates a common frame of reference.

She has bad skin, but always smells nice, like honey or musk.

Dusty tells me most of the stories about Ronald. One night we are invited to a barbecue at William's house. After the other guests have left, William excuses himself.

He has to go in and prepare a few things for tomorrow, he says as his glass eye glows a little in the light from the embers. But we are welcome to stay seated. We can just turn off the lights later if he's gone to bed.

I've had plenty of German curry sausages, salad and semmel and feel pleasantly full, I've also drunk a lot of beer. Mexican ones, admittedly, but still. I'm drowsy and sitting in a comfy lawn chair and Dusty is sitting opposite me. I don't know her that well. It's been a long time since I broke the back of her chair, and tonight we're on the same wavelength, a drowsy and comfortable kind of wavelength. She's also sitting with her eyes half-closed. Her husband is out fishing and she's in no hurry to get home to an empty apartment in Wallingfort.

She has noticed that I hang out with Ronald, she says. Most other people don't like him. But she has always liked him. He has his demons to deal with, she says, and he's managed to make a lot of enemies through the years. For one reason or another. He's also slept with quite a few girls and may even have some offspring here and there that he doesn't want to acknowledge. In his younger days he was very charming. I can vividly imagine that, I say. He's still a handsome man "He's writing a book," she says, "in which he himself is killed by someone at the Department. It's a pretty funny idea, I think."

"Yes," I say. I think so, too.

Psychological Profiles

"Young man!" Ronald shouts. He comes out of the military building and runs after me with his papers under his arm. It's Friday, so he's most likely in a good mood. He's finished the week's classes, it's the weekend, and his retirement is one week closer. I stop and wait until he has caught up with me, out of breath. "Sir," I say and bow slightly.

"I have something very important to tell you," he says in a way that I immediately know he doesn't. He points to an acacia tree on the lawn. "Why don't we sit down?"

"Absolutely."

It's the usual forty degrees, so we're the only ones who've had this idea. We sit down.

"Enjoy your youth!" he says when he has finally come down. "I'll never get up again."

"I'll help you."

"It's a damn shame to grow old. Believe me, I've had some great experiences here on this lawn when I was your age," he says, nudging me in the side with his elbow. "That was back in the happy 60s. They didn't take sexual harassment and that kind of nonsense so seriously."

I nod.

"Look at that one," Ronald says, pointing to a girl in very short hotpants, with long, brown, smooth legs and a short, sleeveless T-shirt. "She shouldn't be allowed to walk there alone like that".

"I agree, but we're not in the '60's anymore."

"Oh, no," he smiles, "I'm sorry."

"Would you like a sip?" he asks and unscrews his cane.

"A small one, sure. I have to go back and prepare."

"Waste of life," he mutters and hands me the cane. We sit in silence and drink, while Ronald watches the students with a dreamy gaze.

"You know how the typical *New York Times* reader is a middle-aged woman," he says after a while, "who works in the canning industry, wears a wig, has three cats and lives in New Hampshire, right?"

"Yeah, something like that. I thought she'd be a little more intellectual, but yes."

"I've been thinking about what the typical scholar looks like. For my book. I think it's a mix of arrogance, striped shirts and cheap leather shoes that have to look more expensive than they are, right?"

"I guess it depends on which faculty they're in."

"That's true. But the one thing they have in common is a desire for power, right? I can't quite make out exactly what you're doing here, but over here everyone has a self-promotional instinct and a loose sense of morality in common. In our system, most people would commit murder to keep their position. Without batting an eye."

"If you say so."

"I can pretty much prove it," he says and takes another sip of his whiskey.

Intrigues

At first, I don't want to get involved in anything, I want to stay as far away as possible from the numerous intrigues. To merely observe all the disputes and laugh about them with Gunther, but that quickly proves impossible. Eventually, the internal problems start to seem significant and it's hard not to get sym and antipathy. And if I talk too long with one of my colleagues, I've automatically chosen a side in the eyes of the others. I can see it in their fake smiles as they pass me in the hallway while I'm talking to one of the unpopular elements. Of which there are many. The stories about the others are numerous: About academic dishonesty, stolen research results, corrupt committee members, fake friends and disloyal colleagues. Sometimes physical appearance is dragged into the suspicion: the slightly too pretty one has used her looks to get ahead (possibly sleeping with her superior), the fat one has abused several students (because she can't get anything else), the well-groomed one is a bit stupid, and the one with the beard is a terrorist.

I talk to Ronald way too much. Many of the

others don't like him, so strategically he's a very bad acquaintance. On the other hand, he is open and polite. He is aware of his stigmatizing effect, so he tries to hide the fact that we are talking. At first I think he's offended, but then I realize it's to protect me. He'll drag me into his office or send emails about where we can meet: the faculty club or a nearby bar. Sometimes, though, we just walk to class, across the lawn, to one of the other buildings. That isn't seen as suspicious by the others.

We're standing still outside the military building when Joy walks by. She's about to bump into me. She's come over from the Germanic Department, so she's probably been at Jenny's to elaborate on her complaints. Ronald is talking about the topography of Kerr's *Noir* trilogy when she spots me. She handles it beautifully. I can see a slight twitch in her eyes, but she smiles and mumbles a hello before changing direction and hurrying towards the parking garage next to the stadium. I follow her with my eyes until Ronald nudges me. "Hey, hey, hey," he says, smiling. "You can't do that. We're not in the '60's."

"No, I know that, too."

"Although sometimes you might want to."

"Are you coming to the department party at Jenny's?" I ask. I don't have the energy to tell him that it was my problem student I was looking at. That it was a thoughtful look, rather than a horny one. Maybe he already knows.

"Not if I can help it. It's usually very painful."

"It would be nice if you did."

"Thank you."

THE DEPARTMENT PARTY AT JENNY'S

I arrive fifteen minutes late. I assume that is the most appropriate time to show up, but they have all already arrived, standing with colored plastic cups filled with welcome drinks containing ice and mint leaves and listening to Jenny, who is giving an informal welcome speech. She pauses for a moment as I enter the room, nods demonstratively: It's so nice that you could find the time to come.

I make my way to the nearest corner to William, who looks up with a wry look and one eye staring lazily at my striped shirt. I pat his upper arm in an awkward gesture that's a little more than a handshake. "There are many challenges ahead of us," Jenny continues her speech in a serious tone, "the small languages are threatened and major cuts have been announced." I spot the bowl with the welcome drink. It's a few meters away from me on a table under the window, and I carefully make my way closer, past Tim McMurian who doesn't greet me. "Thankfully we've received some big donations, so we don't have to be quite as concerned as many others, but it's still going to be a tough year." I take a cup, pour a spoonful of the welcome drink into it and step back, cup in hand. Jenny continues talking about the donation, satisfied students and the quality of our teaching. I take a sip and look around. Sigrun is sitting in the only armchair in the room with her legs crossed so that her pant legs creep up to reveal her purple socks. Her eyes are half-closed and it's hard to tell if she's asleep or just stoned. Paulina is standing next to her, smiling, and Alison next to her. She, like me, is busy observing the other guests and doesn't seem to be paying attention to the speech, her squinty eyes darting around, magnified under the thick lenses of her glasses." I would also like to make an official welcome to our new, talented foreign colleagues," Jenny says, gesturing towards me and Gunther, who must be standing on the opposite side of a wall running halfway across the room. People smile at us. Hermann raises his cup to me in the air and Paulina sort of makes a slight jump. Paulina is stony faced. She's wearing luminescent pants and a tight top and is lost in her own thoughts. "I look forward to spending some nice hours together," Jenny concludes and everyone applauds. I try to put the cup down, but by the time I've found a place for it, it's too late, people have finished clapping and I pick it up again and empty it. I even put the ice cubes in my mouth and crush them.

The atmosphere is a bit awkward, as it is when you fill a room with people who have nothing in common beyond their workplace and who are used to interacting in a safe environment where comments and greetings are already well-established. Here you have to prove your humanity, and people stand around trying to conceal their genitalia behind fig leaves. Tim McMurian is the only one who doesn't let it bother him. He talks loudly to William about his research, asking interested questions so that the whole crowd has to admire his extensive curiosity and broad knowledge. He asks all the right questions and comments on the answers, suggesting titles I've never heard of before.

Gradually a subdued mumbling spreads across the room, the sense of awkwardness slowly vanishes and people manage to come up with suitable entry-lines. I find myself standing next to Jenny's children and I ask them how old they are. Eight and six, they answer before giggling and running out to the kitchen.

Whereupon I stand isolated across from the drinks bowl. The nearest back is Alison's. She looks like a bear in a furry, brown plush dress that reaches her hairy ankles and orthopedic leather sandals. She gestures eagerly, I can see, as she tells Dusty anecdotes from class and laughs out loud at the students' stupidity. I walk over and refill my glass.

I approach Hermann and Tim, who are talking about the similarities between the persecution of the Jews and what Tim calls the crusade against the Muslims. "But you have to understand the situation today is completely different, our historical consciousness alone has crucially changed compared to Germany of the 30s," Hermann says, and I nod in agreement, take a sip of my drink and move on. At the end of the room, on a table facing the kitchen, there are some taco shells and various fillings on small plates, a bowl of strawberries and bowl of carrots and cucumbers. I grab a paper plate and pile a few different things on it. I take my time, carefully considering the choices so that I look busy for as long as possible. Unfortunately, it's quickly eaten and no one approaches me. I stroll around the room and end up next to Sigrun, but she's so stoned that even from across the room it doesn't look like we're having an actual conversation. I walk over to Gunther, who is talking to Jenny about Riefenstahl.

"She was a bitch," he says, and Jenny looks at him, startled.

"I don't want to discuss her guilt, but she was a great artist, her nuba photographs are incomparable."

"But they can't be separated from her guilt."

"Why not?"

"Firstly, because they demonstrate her drive towards well-endowed men, and secondly, because her hypocritical morality and opportunism permeate her work."

"One must be able to consider the work independently of the artist."

"'As long as film critics are Jews, I will never succeed,' she said."

"Unbelievable," I say, pretending to take part in the conversation, but they both just look at me as if they're expecting me to say something more and grow silent. We stand for a while looking down into our empty cups. Then I go back to the punch bowl. Tim and Alison are talking about Ronald, I can detect, but they quickly change the subject when they see me. Alison signals awkwardly to Tim and he turns around and notices me. "My Danish friend," he says loudly and pats me on the shoulder.

"Will you come hear my presentation on Aryan Athletes this Friday at the Humanities Festival?"

Walls with Ears

I meet Ronald on the stairs the next day. "Why didn't you come to the reception?" I ask.

"I hate these things," he says apologetically. "They all wanted me dead and I have similar wishes for them."

"Why? What is it with you?"

"I'll tell you another time. I promise." He smells more strongly of liquor than usual.

"Are you on your way to class?"

"Very well put, my young friend," he says with a smile. "But why don't we grab a beer later? You can't talk here. The walls have ears," he whispers and grimaces like one of those detectives on TV. Just then Gunther comes up the stairs and Ronald winks at me. "See you later," he says.

"What was that all about?" Gunther asks.

"That the walls have ears."

"What are you two up to? People are talking about you, and they aren't always saying nice things. To put it mildly."

"We were just going to have a beer together," I say, looking at him, his round head and knitted eyebrows.

"People always talk in this sort of environment."

Mohitos and Bloody Marys

Conferences are the highlights of the year on campus. They rank right up there with Christmas, Thanksgiving and Hanukkah. Or a carnival. They're an opportunity to finally kiss the new exchange student, to drink your brains out with some good old colleagues from other universities who pose no threat to your hard-won status. Networking is key, and social skills are rewarded in the right away.

Presentations are an alibi for buffets, drinks and fornication. Of course, you couldn't do without them, because then you wouldn't have anything to belittle, or use as convenient topical opening lines when you want to get into the pants of that cute redhead from UC Berkeley.

On the first day, everybody behaves in a civilized manner. You meet at the buffet and make small talk. You greet old friends. You talk about your research, your family and hometown, and you pretend to be interested in the main topic of the conference or the keynote speaker's opening lecture (an anorexic author from Sweden). You nod and listen to your old colleagues' similar stories, are your children really that old already? I remember when they were no bigger than a bag of chips.

It lasts until the evening, which is when the usual party animals finally start to get into the swing of things. They invite each other over for drinks in their rooms and entice the boring ones to join them, because there could be some great stories for next year's conference if you manage to drink them under the table or lure them in bed with you. You have taken the whole arsenal with you, as you mix Mohitos, Bloody Marys and Sex on the Beach, while gradually becoming increasingly cheerful, the comments becoming more frivolous and perfidious, and a little later you all come rushing out, running and screaming through the hallway, knocking chairs over and writing naughty things on the blackboards in the meeting rooms. A few of the older professors smear toothpaste on the door handles, giggling and reminiscing about the childhood they never had, to later chase the girls at the makeshift disco which has been set up in the hotel restaurant. A few try to make conversation at the small tables along the wall, but it's hard to make themselves heard as a newly hired Harvard professor keeps cranking up the volume, playing *YMCA* and *All That She Wants* at full blast, while his colleague sings loudly along to the songs.

I myself am cornered by a Danish lecturer from Grenå, who has spent the first half of the evening talking about her husband and children, and is now spending the second half making out with me.

A SESSION IN MORPHOLOGY

She must have snuck up on me. I've just been talking to Gunther about his late-night encounter with a freshman, first at the cowboy bar downtown, then in the back of his pickup truck. When I turn around, there she is. She's not that pretty, a little too thin, but with nice breasts and a firm, slightly skinny behind. "Hi," she says, but that's all she says, and even though I don't feel like it, I naturally answer "Hi," without smiling, without seeming too inviting, yet still inviting enough for her to stick around.

"I'm a PhD fellow at the department," she says. "I don't think we've met." She's a redhead with freckles and glasses, and she could be pretty if it weren't for her nerdy attitude and her thin, slightly neglected look. She's wearing a cowboy skirt and clogs. Later I find out she kisses well and looks exceptionally good without clothes on, that she actually also looks good on my couch when she lies naked on her back with her legs spread apart. But that's not until later. First we have to go through an awkward conversation about our research goals and results, Germany, where she is originally from, and briefly say goodbye before we meet again after a long conference day over some quarter sandwiches with crab salad and cucumber.

She wants to attend a talk on morphology and syntax, while I've just decided to listen to some of our own colleagues from the department. I declined the offer of presenting something myself because I thought I had enough to see to just settling down into things, but Gunther has decided to dive right into it and is going to talk about "Islands as a Mental State" in his broken American English. His language doesn't bother him, but you can see a few patches of perspiration forming under his armpits as he gesticulates wildly or uses primitive phrases to draw our attention to particularly interesting islands to which he points with a stick. Afterwards, Tim McMurian talks about Aryan Athletes, looking confident and exhibiting professorial energy as he does so. Dusty presents a post-modern and entertaining approach to unwritten stories and the fear of the white piece of paper. She starts by telling how her niece came to her one day and gave her a piece of white paper. She was fascinated by the purity of the paper and didn't want to draw over it, but if she had wanted to, she would have drawn a princess and a dragon. Dusty holds up the paper, summarizes Blixen's points of "The blank page," but still ends up in Hitler's diaries, Nazi paratexts and lost documents.

Finally, Ronald talks about German crime literature after the War. He has been listening attentively to the others, nodding encouragingly and taking notes down on a pad. According to the program, which I am sitting with in my lap, he is going to talk about crime literature, but the title has the usual catchy tone: "The Death of a Professor—A Farewell Lecture." It's very elegant and it's the first time I actually get a chance to see him in action.

His point of departure is Philip Kerr, in Berlin, just before the 1936 Olympic Games, but then you quickly realize it's an analogy. That the Nazi setting could be transferred to the Department, and that the detective Bernhard Gunther might as well be called Ronald Keller. But nothing is said in direct terms, everything is implied, and you have to know something about the circumstances to be able to make the connection, that the Nazi archives are, in fact, the research results of our colleagues, and Bernhard's revelations are Ronald's struggles. I look around at the audience, and notice the only ones laughing are those outside of the department. Our colleagues from the department are all sitting stone-faced and staring, Alison has drops of sweat on her moustache and her eyes are flashing, Jenny is looking down at the floor and Tim is sitting back with his arms crossed, staring up at Ronald without changing his expression. Only Hermann seems to be enjoying himself a little. He smiles several times under his leather cap and Hitler mustache as he looks around.

Ronald ends by telling some anecdotes from his long life in academia. They are very harmless. "This is the last time I'll be appearing at a conference," he says, "and I'm really glad it could be here at the University where I've worked most of my life. I've been here on a daily basis for over forty years," he makes a pause for effect and looks out at his audience, "but I won't miss you for a second." He says it so disarmingly that most of the audience laughs. Afterwards, we politely applaud. I can see that Ronald is kind of falling apart. The cheerful expression he had a moment ago leaves his face and he looks old and like he's on the run. It has been a huge effort for him to give his last speech, and it has been imperative for him to deliver it well. I wave up to him, but he doesn't register it. He's in a completely different place. He has just said goodbye to this world.

RONALD'S DEATH

Of course, I'm the one who finds him. Otherwise, I guess I wouldn't be a convincing protagonist. It's evening and most people have gone home when I go to see if Gunther has left. He hasn't. I'm in a strange mood and can't seem to calm down. For the last couple of hours my eyes have been unable to focus on the screen and I've been fidgeting impatiently in my chair, checking the news online every two minutes and walk round the office a few times.

Without a second thought, I go and knock on Tim's door with the toppling piles of books. I wouldn't normally do that, but today is not normal. If it were, Tim would be inside behind his piles working on something about doping and rogue athletes. He has nothing to come home to, so he stays in the office pretty much every day until the evening.

I stand still and listen. There is not a sound. A hiss from the air conditioning, a bird scratching outside a window, and shortly afterwards a door slamming downstairs, but no sign of life on this floor. Usually, there's always someone grading final assignments or writing the last paragraph of a revolutionary article about an unknown Nazi author.

I walk down the hallway and turn the corner to go back to my office. I might as well collect my things and go home, maybe get drunk alone, watch a DVD and go to bed. But then, to my delight, I realize that Ronald's door is open. A drink with Ronald at a nearby café would suit my mood perfectly, so I go and knock on the half-open door. No answer.

"Ronald," I call, pushing the door with my foot.

He's lying on the floor with blood running out of his mouth and his eyes turned towards the sky outside the far window. *Mein Kampf* lies next to him on the floor with blood on its stiff back.

3

"There are more hygienic ways of cleansing a man's ears than using a nine millimeter projectile"
from *March Violets* by Philip Kerr

"Reality can be arranged in such a way that it resembles randomness."
from *Contemplated Thoughts* by W. Schreibner

Smell of Alcohol

Suddenly, everything changes and the creepiness sneaks up on me from the hallway. There is an inexplicable change in the surroundings, as if ignorance had so far spared me from anything scary. By instinct, I make sure no one is in the hallway, stand and listen for a moment before closing the door. I turn back to Ronald. If it weren't so tragic, it would almost be too ironic, considering he wanted to kill himself in his novel. But who the hell would kill him in real life? He didn't have many friends, and at his farewell lecture I myself saw how he was able to turn everybody against him. Several times I have heard colleagues speak unfavorably about him, but never outright hatefully, it was always just the usual academic back-stabbing. It's hard to work in this world for so long a time without having a falling out with someone at some point.

He looks old as he lies there on the floor. His hair is dry and gray, and his skin resembles parchment and is wrinkly. But he also looks serene, and it's almost as if a smile is breaking out on his face. He had mellowed out somewhat in his old age, several of his colleagues have told me. In his younger years, he was a real bon vivant, cynic and womanizer. In his older days, he resigned himself to living quietly with his four dogs and loved to ironize life. A little too often he smelled of booze when he meekly trudged across the square to teach, but that's no reason to kill him. Of course, the hatred could have gone back further and have been fueled further since then.

I immediately rule out suicide, even though it would almost be like the ironist killing himself in order to realize his fiction; to see if his theory would hold true and the latent murderer would reveal himself. But he would have had more than enough trouble killing himself with *Mein Kampf*. The blow has hit him with great force in the forehead, causing him to fall backwards and slam the back of his head into the floor. He must have bitten his tongue in the fall, where else would all that blood come from? I bend over him and look at his sad figure. He still reeks of alcohol, possibly whiskey, but it's hard to define the smell exactly, because it also smells of blood, sweat and urine. His skin is still damp and there's a wet spot in his pants, so it can't have been long since he died.

I sit down next to the body, leaning against a bookcase.

It's probably not wise to leave so many fingerprints at a crime scene, but I'm not thinking clearly at the moment. To put it mildly. I have a funny feeling in my stomach and am feeling slightly nauseous, if I listen, I can almost hear my insides crashing. At the same time it feels as if the connection from my head has been cut off. It doesn't notify the body of physical collapse, crying or nervous spasms. It maintains normality. It thinks, I think. It thinks to keep emotions at bay.

Ronald's office is quite large. It has three casement windows, two facing the neighboring building and one facing the park where the acacia trees are currently in bloom. I can't see that from here, but I know it. Earlier today I had lunch on the lawn with Gunther, a portion of salad with chicken and plenty of dressing. Now it's dark, and besides, I'm sitting down, so I have to envision the blossoming of the trees. I can, however, see a pale moon through one window and a dull lamp mounted on the building opposite, casting a dim light on Ronald.

Along the wall behind me and under the two windows are some dark rosewood bookcases, full of books and folders and a few piles of loose slips of paper. The desk extends from the wall, facing one of the windows. There's a computer in the middle of it, an old Macintosh with its characteristically curved screen, and next to it are scattered papers, a paper cup from Starbucks, three cheap pens and an open bag of cookies. Behind the table is a high-backed desk chair and in front of it are two low chairs. They are mainly for students, but I have also sat in them several times where we've talked about life and death, literature and music. He loved music, Bruckner and Wagner in particular, but he would also occasionally follow the newer music scene. In general, he was a curious person, and thus exhibited very little self-importance. He had an eye for something other than himself, and his nihilistic outlook allowed him to view the world more impartially than most of his biased colleagues. He was easy to talk to, never judgmental and always ready to go off on tangents with a twinkle in his eye.

The building is still completely silent. It must be around nine o'clock. You can hear the air conditioner whirring, but otherwise there's not a sound. I swallow and am surprised by the noise. Once you get used to silence, the slightest noise can be anxiety-provoking. It's reminiscent of when you were watching horror movies as a child and didn't dare turn under your crinkling blanket afterwards. What if the killer is still around and my noisy swallowing sounds summon him? I manage to pull myself together, get up and walk over to the desk.

ACADEMIC FREEDOM

I don't actually know what Ronald was researching, but I do know that he didn't publish much. He got tenureship at a time when the requirements were different than today. To get tenureship today, you have to publish a lot during the five years you are actually under review. The system was introduced to ensure academic freedom, because once you get tenureship, you are virtually impossible to get rid of, so you don't have to fear for your career when you vocally criticize various issues. But it can also act as a sleeping pillow because, strictly speaking, you don't have to produce anything after you've gotten tenureship. Furthermore, the review process ensnares people into toxic networks because you risk becoming colleagues with the very people who are involved in employing and determining your eligibility for tenureship, the process of which is grueling in itself. Several of my younger colleagues look like deep-sea fish on land on the rare occasions that I see them. Their eyes are wide as they stare into the daylight while telling me how many articles they still need to write. Fortunately, as a guest lecturer, I'm outside the system, and it's been many years since Ronald had to go through that mill, so he didn't have to produce anything and could enjoy his retirement years in advancement. He was due to retire next summer and he was looking forward to it like a little kid who is looking forward to Christmas. Then he would finally write his great novel about academia and end up killing himself in an ironic maneuver that would expose his colleagues as scheming egotists.

The papers on the table are covered in illegible scribblings for the class. Ronald taught European crime fiction and could talk for hours on end about Agatha Christie, Arthur Conan Doyle and Philip Kerr, especially the latter's Berlin *Noir* trilogy. We talked about them on the days we taught in the same building and walked together across the square. This was also where we would take a sip of his whiskey hidden in his cane. "You really need to read Philip Kerr," he would say, "his descriptions of places are amazing. It's like being in Berlin itself. I've checked several of the locations and they're absolutely accurate." The trilogy is set in Berlin before, during and after the War, but was written in the '80's, so in terms of the Department, he was ultramodern. His shelves are filled with crime novels and reference books in that genre, as well as creative writing manuals on how to write novels, which must have been for personal use.

The computer on the table is on. It shows a slideshow of himself, his dogs and his farm in the countryside. In one of the pictures he is standing in front of a barn and smiling, in another on a pier wearing short shorts and no shirt. He looks fit for hs age. There is no one else in the photos. I nudge the mouse and the slides give way to an open document he must have been working on when he was so brutally interrupted. I pull the office chair over to the desk and sit down in front of the screen.

The document turns out to be notes for his novel, neatly recorded in an Excel spreadsheet. Characters, important points in the plot, suspense curves. He has added some three-digit numbers next to several of the notes. I look at them but can't make sense of them. It's clear that they refer to something, but without a key, they don't make sense. I minimize the document so that it folds into a small bar at the bottom of the page. Underneath are several open windows posted on the

University's website, on pages about Native American tribes in Arizona and historical revisionism. The last one is open on a database of crime novels.

I stop while in the midst of reading. I think I hear noises outside the door, but the background hum of the fan makes me uncertain. The sound of shuffling footsteps that have just stopped. When I look over, I think I see a shadow under the door, reaching across the floor, and my skin starts to tingle. I hold my breath in order to better be able to listen, but the footsteps have stopped—and the shadow isn't moving, so maybe it's nothing. Then my heart suddenly stops momentarily as the door handle slowly moves downwards. The person on the other side hesitates, then the handle goes back up. The shadow falls under the door, but then its source turns and heads down the hallway towards the stairs. I hear the footsteps disappear and a click sound as the door to the stairway opens, followed by a loud slam as it shuts. I go to the window to see who is going out of the front door, but there is no one. Either the person is still up here or he has taken the back exit. I sit back in my chair.

I've already subconsciously told myself that I don't

dare leave the office. For a moment I consider calling the police, but something stops me. Possibly the thought of my fingerprints, which are now all over the room, on the corpse, the books, the table and the keyboard. Possibly the silence that I don't want to break. I lean back in the chair, bring my fingertips together in front of my chest and look around. A cowboy hat is lying on top of one of the shelves, next to some folded maps. On the shelf below are a number of small glass figurines, which is the only thing that signals some kind of homey coziness. Finally, I look down at Ronald, who has already started to smell foul. It was only just a few days ago that we met in the faculty club and talked about long-legged girls, and now he's lying here, smelling foul. Life is a funny thing. I look at the slides that have started to run across the screen again, then I open a drawer in the desk and, not so surprisingly, discover a bottle of whiskey, as well as some pens and lined notepads.

I pull the cork off the bottle and take a sip of the whiskey. Then I lean forward, open a new window onto a search page and type: Ronald Keller.

A Stale Past Life

Ronald, as mentioned, was very much looking forward to retirement. He started almost every conversation with that topic. As if to apologize for the fact that he was still lingering at the University like a discarded relic of the past, an alcoholic lame duck. He wasn't comfortable with the students, he said, the distance had become too great, and every day he just hoped they wouldn't ask him too many questions. That he could just conduct a lecture and hopefully thereby infect the young people with his passion for literature. I don't know if the students liked him, but they probably sensed his insecurity. They can usually smell that right away.

There are over 15,000 hits, but I can tell right away that not all of them are about my Ronald. However, a couple of the first ones are and refer to some of his articles written in the '60's. He hasn't written any books, but he has written a number of articles and forewords, and he has edited a single book on post-war German crime novels.

On the Department's own website, I find a profile

he presumably wrote himself. He graduated from Ohio University, it says, from which he attained a Master of Fine Arts. Since then, he has taught at various universities in the US. First at some rather inferior private colleges such as "Gustavus Adolphus College," "St. Olaf College," "Macalester College," which are all religiously based. From there he suddenly jumped to the country's largest university, where he has remained ever since. There's nothing in his list of publications to justify the jump, but he may very well have known someone who was already teaching in the department. He became Assistant Professor in 1967 and Associate Professor five years later.

Over the years, he has written a number of journal articles, including "The Position of Fiction in Post-War Germany," "Boundaries in the Crime Novel, with an Emphasis on Works by Milne and Kerr," and "The Face of Hitler—a Comparative Analysis of the Führer's Imprint on Contemporary Texts." So he has also sailed the Nazi galley. It doesn't surprise me.

I close the document and look at his virtual desktop. There are several folders and documents on it. Most of them have something to do with teaching: report cards, notes, handouts, reading lists and lesson plans on broad topics like "The European Novel" or "The World's Scariest Movies and Books." It's all about selling the product and attracting students. You can see there is some sort of system, but for an outsider, it's difficult to grasp. Each folder contains subfolders, which in turn contain even more subfolders. It's a Chinese box system. Ronald loved systems, puzzles and playing with complicated rules. One of the first times we had a beer together, he told me hat he had some old friends he played with. It could be anything from new versions of tennis to homemade board games and philosophical treasure hunts. It sounded nice, I thought. Sometimes he would tell me a riddle on the way across the lawn to class: "If you can solve this one, young man, I'll buy you a beer after class," and I could spend half my brain activity solving it while I was teaching.

Apart from the notes for the novel, it seems that the vast majority of the documents on the computer are related to teaching and research. There is also a folder of letters, but apparently none of them are addressed to anyone from the department. I remember he once told me he had rented an office where he was writing his novel. He had collected a lot of material, he said, and it would take up too much space in the office. Besides, it was nice to separate the two things. Even though his office wasn't that charming, I think it was in a basement somewhere in the University. I would no doubt get to see it sometime, he said.

I open the desk drawers and find a sea of envelopes, clips, napkins, pens, but nothing of immediate value to me. Then I freeze. On one of the envelopes my name is written in red capital letters. I recognize Ronald's slightly trembling handwriting. Underneath, he has added my address in regular ballpoint pen. I pick up the envelope. It's not stamped, so he must have expected to deliver it to me personally, but why the address? I turn it over a few times before opening. It feels all wrong, but that's kind of the point.

The envelope contains a manuscript, but there's a note stuck on it: "Greetings from the realm of the dead," it simply says, "I hope you like it." "Arrival," it says at the top of the page.

He arrives in Houston late at night. He's tired. He hasn't slept for almost two days and is in a glass bubble of jet lag and plugged ears. He steps out onto the floating landing tunnel, which has just been attached to the plane like a mechanical measuring inch worm. It gives way ominously. The warm, humid air of an early evening penetrates through the cracks and he breathes heavily. Through the small windows he can see the setting sun. It's a little after five o'clock.

It could be anyone, but it's not. I don't realize it at first, but then I suddenly realize it's about me. Of course, it's not a transcript of reality, but what is? The important thing is that I recognize myself—and the stories I've been telling Ronald over the past few months. Suddenly I understand why he asked so many questions, seemed so curious, listened so attentively. His welcoming curiosity served a purpose, and his curiosity was also due to professional interest. He was gathering information for his story.

I don't know why he has chosen me as the main character in his novel, but it's clear that despite the circumstances, I can't help but read on. I have to see what Ronald's imagination has gotten me into. Perhaps it might also explain how I ended up here, next to a smelly corpse in an abandoned Department somewhere in Texas. If this were fiction, Ronald's fiction, I would now be at the beginning of the novel, where he himself is dead and the investigation is about to begin.

The script starts with my arrival in Houston, the trip with Angelina in a kind of caricatured road movie with dramatic highlights, but then it all develops in a somewhat unrealistic direction, turning into an underground trip through a sewer with a thin-haired guy in overalls. I myself, my fictional doppelganger, ends up in what must be the first part, tied up in a dark room underground. It's not great literature, but in Ronald's defense, the script is not finished. In places, the language lags a little, but it can be seen as a sketch. Later, he would probably go back and smooth out the rough edges. "To be continued," it ends, and below that Ronald has added: "The ending is up to you" and a little smiley face. I send a small curse in his direction.

In some notes at the bottom of the page, he mentions the secret door I dreamt about. But I can't remember if I told him about the dream or if he may have had a parallel experience. Or if the door actually exists. And now I'm no longer sure if I'm the one who killed Ronald. In a flash, I see myself holding *Mein Kampf* raised high above my head a few meters on the floor in front of me. I close my eyes and try to control my breathing. This is madness. Why would I kill Ronald, I think, looking down at my shaking hands. Why would anyone?

A Sloppy Shave

After sitting like this for a while, I collect myself. I straighten up in the office chair and stare blankly into space. All I really wanted to do was ask Ronald out for a drink, and now I'm sitting here. Without really knowing how I ended up here, and, more specifically, without having any idea how I'm going to get out of here.

I get up, stand for a while and look out across the lawn, which is halfway covered in darkness. It's starry, I see, and it's actually very nice to be reminded of the outside world. But then I see a figure over by the history building looking across towards me, and I quickly step away from the window.

"To be continued," I think. He obviously knew I would get the manuscript after his death, which of course also means he knew he was going to die. I wonder if he also knew how? Does the sequel exist somewhere? And if so, what role do I play in it?

I lie down on the floor next to Ronald and stare up into the air. I don't know what good this will do, but it is the best thing I can come up with. Would it be better that I scream, run around the office and wring my hands? I think. That I cry?

There's just enough room for both of us on the floor between desk and door. I turn on my side and look at my friend, the corpse. He's lying on his back, but his face is turned towards me, staring straight at me with his quiet smile. He hasn't shaved properly under his chin, I note. He is otherwise relatively clean-shaven, but in several places there are still some long stubbles. Would he have made more of an effort if he had known it was his last shave? I reach out my hand, but still don't have the courage to touch him. I pull back my hand, but then I gather all my courage and close his eyes. I don't know what I had imagined, but it's easier than I thought. He's still warm and his skin is soft. His eyes almost close on their own. Still, it's uncomfortable and my pulse starts pounding in my temples.

Who murdered you? Who the hell knocked you out with *Mein Kampf* and left you in your own bodily fluids on the floor for a Danish guest lecturer to find? He still stinks, but I must be getting used to it. It no longer seems so nauseating. I sit up and try to concentrate, but my mind is running feverishly in circles. One image follows the next at a furious pace, Dusty, Sigrun, Alison, Tim alternating with the book in their hands, Ronald on the floor, Gunther's sarcastic voice, chanting something about guilt, punishment and crossing boundaries. It makes sense, I say to myself, but the next moment I've forgotten how. I lie down again. It must be someone from the Department, is the last thing I think before I fall asleep.

RONALD'S EYES

I wake up on the floor with an uneasy feeling in my stomach. It takes ten seconds to remember where I am and another ten to remember what happened. My head and neck hurt. I must have been sleeping in an awkward position, and now my eyes are gritty and my head is heavy, but despite Ronald's lifeless presence, the office has lost some of its eeriness, and I realize it would be stupid to stay here too long.

It's still night, but the darkness has a different quality. The night has tipped towards morning, but I don't know what time it is. I must have left my watch in the office. I get up and walk towards the door. It's darker than when I fell asleep, it seems, and I can only make out Ronald's dead form on the floor in front of me. His eyes shine towards me. It's as if they follow me as I walk towards the door. I am a rational thinking being, I think, so this shouldn't scare me. On the other hand, I can't for the life of me remember turning off the lights in the office, and Ronald's eyes still follow me as I walk across him and walk to the door, which I hesitantly open.

The hallway is resoundingly empty. A sleepy lamp casts a yellow light across one wall and half of the floor. The rest is in darkness, and I know you have to go to the stairway to turn on the real light. There could be many criminals hiding in the shadows, I think, but I'm strangely indifferent. Still, I hesitate, listening with bated breath before moving along the hallway towards the door to the stairs. Once, I stop. It's as if someone puts their feet on the floor in sync with mine, and I'm pretty sure I can hear a delayed footstep as mine stops. Maybe it's the echo of my own footsteps, or my pulse beating loudly against my temple again. I no longer feel certain of anything.

I open the door to the hallway. It's loud. The door handle squeeches as I push it down and the door squeaks improbably loud as I force it open. I wait until the door slams shut and listen out into the darkness. Now I am no longer in doubt: Footsteps! I can't tell if they're coming from above or below until someone presses down the door handle behind me and my pounding pulse stops. The world is suddenly moving in slow motion: I scream distortedly and hurl myself down the stairs, floating in the air for a long time before landing on the stairs, take off again and hit the landing. I slowly turn my head at the next landing and see the door open, but don't have time to see anyone's face before I rush further down the stairs. The door on the floor below is open and I run into the hallway and towards the exit on the right, past the Coke machine and into the door next to it, which doesn't lead out, but down. The footsteps behind me get closer and so the choice has been made, and I continue down into the darkness, to a basement full of archive boxes and listening equipment and through a small door I slam shut behind me. A gurgling sound in the darkness behind me makes me turn around and I see a man lying bound and gagged on the floor. When he looks up, I can see it's me. Then the door is torn open and Tim McMurian enters holding *Mein Kampf* raised above his head .

In Reality

Iwake up on the floor with an uneasy feeling in my stomach. It takes ten seconds to remember where I am and another ten to remember what happened. My head and neck hurt. I must have been lying in an awkward position in the chair, sleeping, and now my eyes are gritty and my head is heavy. I hate ambiguous dreams, but now the office looks like it did when I fell asleep. The lights are on, Ronald's eyes are closed and it's dark outside. I take these as sure indicators of reality.

I sit up and massage my eyebrows. I look out into the office. I stretch. I think about my hopeless situation, and even in my waking state I can see the sense in leaving the office before morning. So I get up and walk towards the door when I spot a pack of handkerchiefs on the shelf. I take one, unfold it and wipe off the places I remember leaving my fingerprints. Good thinking, I think. I open the door with the handkerchief and wipe the handle on the outside before closing it again. I catch a glimpse of Ronald's peaceful figure before the door closes completely. The wet spot in his pants has dried up and the blood has stopped flowing. Now it lies in an unreal stain on the floor next to his ear.

The hallway light is on and it's not as creepy as I had feared.

No footsteps, no abnormal noises, no sign of criminals. I walk down the hallway towards my office, turn down the small passage, past the broom closet and fumblingly open the door to my small office as my pulse races wildly. I slam it behind me and feel the blood pounding against my temple. I stand like that for a while. Then I sit down in my desk chair and put my legs up on the edge of the desk. For some reason that calms me. I look at the Dannebrog on the table, at the row of kings, at the Crown Prince and Mary and the Hans Christian Andersen calendar hanging on the wall, at the green chairs opposite. I think of the Korean student who stripped in one of them some time ago...

So, now what? I think. My heart is still beating rapidly and my mouth is dry. There's a drop of lukewarm soda in a plastic cup on my desk, and I drink it. Then I sit for a while, biting the rim of the cup until it cracks. I get up and walk over to the computer, which is on a desk along the other wall, sit down in the high-backed desk chair, whose armrests have been torn to shreds by my predecessors, and absent-mindedly start surfing. First something about Ronald, then news and dubious home videos, stars and illustrated sports pages. A few times I doze off, but then I wake up shortly afterwards and in so doing wake up the computer, which is dozing behind the screensaver. Even though there are no windows in the office, I have a clear sense it is night: the silence, the sense of exhaustion, the computer's clock, but also the unidentifiable quality of the room.

My brain seems to have stalled. I think of Ronald several times, and the sight of him lying on the floor is imprinted in my memory. But I don't try to understand, don't process the impressions, just let the images pass by my mind's eye as I read the news and comics, watch movies and music videos without sound. That's how the time passes until morning. I can hear the door open and close a few times and some muffled voices outside.

Around nine o'clock I sneak out. I try to walk as normally as possible, first upstairs to the bathroom to wash up, then downstairs to get a Coke. I manage to get back to the office without saying hello to anyone.

Two Minutes of Silence

I don't have to teach until noon, so I stay in the office with the door ajar, as I normally would. A little later I go to check the mail and say hello to Emily and a couple of the others, get coffee and talk to Jenny. It's a strange feeling to pretend to be normal when not so long ago you were sleeping next to a corpse.

There's a nervous atmosphere in the Department, but at the same time it's as if Ronald never existed. No one mentions him, but I know he's been discovered because the door to his office is open and I've seen some forensic technicians walking up and down the corridors in coveralls and carrying suitcases full of technical equipment. Later that day, we get an email from Jenny, briefly explaining that Ronald has died. The cause is unknown, but the Department will honor his memory with a two-minute silence before the faculty meeting on Friday. And she will get back to us when she knows when he will be buried. It's all very tragic, she writes, but you get the feeling that it is not that tragic. She might as well have reminded us of the upcoming lecture on "Gender Aspects of Riefenstahl's Triumpf des Willens."

On my way to Gunther, I meet both Dusty, who passes by without saying hello, and Tim, who is sitting on the couch in the hallway with a student. He looks up at me, but doesn't say hello either.

Gunther immediately starts recounting the night's escapades as soon as he spots me. This time it's a poor Chinese guy of 21, something about a cargo bike and a deserted trail down by the river.

"Didn't you hear Ronald died?" I ask.

"Yeah, yeah. I just read Jenny's email. Why?"

"He was hit on the head with *Mein Kampf*," I say in an attempt to get through to him.

"Oh." He looks at me uncomprehendingly. "Why don't we go get a cup of coffee? I haven't had any coffee at all today. I need coffee. I was up half the night with that Chinese guy. It was crazy. He was so short that he could give me a blow job standing up."

We walk into the office, past Tim, who still doesn't say hello, and through the door to Emily, who is painting her nails while talking on the phone. I greet her loudly and she lights up in a fake smile that lasts until she spots us. Then it freezes and she devotes her full attention to the phone, the Spanish-speaking listener on the other end: "Professeur" and "muerte" I hear. Her bunch of keys is next to her on the table. I remember it coming up at some of the faculty meetings why the administrative staff should have access to our offices when we, the professors, don't have access to the office after hours. I don't remember what the explanation was, but it didn't help to calm things down.

Just then, Jenny comes out of her office behind Emily. She looks excited. Through the door I can see Tim McMurian and a blonde woman I don't recognize because her back is turned. Her hair doesn't look real. It's a little too light, gathered in a split ponytail with a red elastic. Jenny tries to compose herself, smiles strainedly at us, but turns to Emily, who quickly puts the phone down on the table.

"Milk and cream?" Gunther asks.

"Yes. Can you take it to your office? I have to go to the restroom." At least I need to collect my thoughts. Gunther is fumbling ungracefully with the funnel which is in a cup and he has moved the pot. He nods.

I walk out into the hallway and take a turn around the horseshoe on our floor before heading upstairs.

Several of the doors are ajar. Gunther's, Dusty's, Tim's and Alison's. They're all here, but you can't see any of them, and there's no visible commotion, even though one of their colleagues lies dead a few meters away from them. Still, I sense there is life behind the doors, and if I walk past slowly, I can hear voices in some places. Tim is talking on the phone in broken German and Dusty is apparently visiting Sigrun. Through the door I catch a few words, and it's about Ronald: "I helped hire him," Sigrun says, "even though he wasn't really suited for the job. He had connections and there was pressure on us to take him on. It was the same with the permanent position. He was probably on the borderline and might have been hired, but we were told he had to be hired. Someone was afraid of him. He had knowledge that made him valuable." Dusty replies something that I don't pick up on. Her words are harder to decipher through the door, she speaks at a completely different frequency than Sigrun and also a lot lower. "I didn't really know him," she finishes louder.

"He brought it on himself," Sigrun says, but then a door closes around the corner and some footsteps approach, so I continue down the hallway and up to

224

the second-floor restroom. I notice the door to Ronald's office is now closed and sealed with police tape.

One of the graduate students is brushing his teeth at the sink. His parents are both dentists, and he brushes his teeth every time he takes a bite of something. A few minutes after eating a burrito or a bagel, he discreetly disappears into the restroom with his little toilet bag. I greet him with a nod before I wash my hands and go out.

Gunther is gone when I get back to the office. I check the kitchen, the copying room and the mail room just to be sure. As I'm about to leave, I hear shouting from the opposite side and go over. It's Alison. Sometimes she freaks out and her colleagues treat her like an armour piercing bomb with a faulty trigger.

Apparently, she has placed a series of videos about the Second World War and Leni Riefenstahl on a table at the reception. On top of them, she has placed a note that reads: "Touch these and die!" At some point, Jenny got tired of looking at both the videos and the sign and asked the student assistant to put them back in place. His name is Sam and he's half Irish and, according to my Dutch friend, a closet gay. Alison catches him in the middle of the act. He has collected the videos in a box and is now distributing them on the shelves in the copying room according to an ingenious system.

"What are you doing?" she screams, running to the box. "My videos."

"I'm putting them back," Sam says matter-of-factly. "Don't you fucking put them back, you imbecilic idiot. I specifically told you that no one was to touch them." She's on the verge of tears, her voice quivering with anger, but also with suppressed whining. When Jenny comes in a moment later on account of the noise, Alison is in a frenzy. She's started pushing Sam and throwing videos he's just put in place on the floor. "Those are my videos," she sobs. "My videos!" She looks at Jenny with red eyes. "I kept them in a very specific order." Jenny looks at the two of them and hesitantly takes a step forward, but doesn't say anything. They look at each other. Something is going on that I can't decipher, but it must have been brewing for some time. "Why don't we, for Ronald's sake, try to be civilized?" Jenny asks. Alison looks startled at first. Then she walks towards Jenny while whispering: "What the hell are you talking about? You have no idea who he was and who you're setting yourself up against." She strides past her before Jenny can react. I'm not sure she wants to respond either. I think she must have built up most of her courage when she spoke last time. I smile at her awkwardly after Alison has walked past me. I want to say something to defuse the tense situation and to distract from the fact that I've just seen the Head of the Department being scolded by one of her employees, but I don't have the energy to think of anything. My head is resoundingly empty, and both it and my shoulders ache. Luckily, Emily comes to my rescue. She comes in and asks Jenny in her sweet voice what happened and if she could have helped with anything

I take the opportunity to withdraw. What's more, I get an idea. With a determination that surprises myself, I grab Emily's keys on my way out. I put them in my pocket and head back into the mail room. It takes less than half a minute. I wait until Emily is back in her seat before I head out. I make an effort to greet her so that she can't escape noticing it.

GUNTHER'S OFFICE

Gunther has gone back to his office. He's on the phone with his German boyfriend and signals for me to sit down when he sees me in the doorway. He points to a cup of coffee on the table and I sit down and drink it. It tastes like sweet milk, but it's a murky brown so that way it has a faint resemblance of real coffee.

Gunther's office is unusually boring. There's an empty bookcase at one end, a large brown desk with a German flag on it given to him by his boyfriend the last time he visited, an office chair, a computer desk and two visitor chairs. He has absolutely no aesthetic sense and he couldn't care less. As a gay man, he may feel at times obligated to feign caring about such things, but when he is with me he lets it all hang out. His boyfriend is really into that sort of thing, so Gunther lets him take care of it. His boyfriend buys flowers and blankets and cushions when he's here, but it all inexplicably disappears when he's gone. The flowers are removed and the cushions fall behind his sofa at home and are never retrieved.

Gunther has hung up the phone and I have told him once again I was in Ronald's office last night. That I saw him dead, hit over the head with *Mein Kampf*, that I heard footsteps, but now I don't know how much was a dream and how much reality. For example, I'm not entirely sure I'm not the one who did it.

"But why would you have done that?" he asks. "And why would you use Hitler's memoirs? You could have used the party program of the Danish People's Party or Saxo's *Chronicle of Denmark*. But *Mein Kampf*?" I'm always impressed by how well he keeps up with Danish affairs.

"I don't know. But I also don't know why I stayed in the office for so long. Suddenly it was like I was there. Like I woke up in there without knowing how I got there."

"But you liked Ronald. Weren't you just overwhelmed when you found him and went into a kind of shock?"

"Maybe. Another strange thing is that he was writing a book in which he himself was killed and in which I play the main character. I found the first part in his desk drawer."

Gunther takes a sip of his coffee and makes a face. "Shitty American coffee," he snarls. Then he looks at me, pretending to be serious. "That does sound strange."

"Also that no one talks about him. Jenny just sends out a clinical email and I just saw Alison freaking out in the copy room. There's nothing unusual about that, of course."

"Who could have done this?" he asks. "I actually heard your name mentioned in Jenny's office after you left. Tim was in there with a woman I didn't know and said something about suspicious behavior, but I didn't relate it to Ronald. I just thought, well, yeah, you are suspicious. In a good way, that is," he adds with a smile. "We are foreigners here in the age of the war against terror. We actually deserve to wear fancy little stars on our chests." I nod.

"Should we drink a cup of coffee later?" he asks. "Then we can talk about who we should nail for the murder. I need to prepare a little bit before my next class in an hour. I still need to correct a couple of essays, but I'll think about the situation in the meantime."

He gestures toward the door to shoo me out. Politeness has never been his forte.

STRATEGIES

I myself teach at 2 p.m. It takes a lot before you start canceling routines, and it gives you a sense of security to practice irregular verbs and subordinating conjunctions while the world around you is crashing. I always thought you would find other strategies if you were under pressure, but you don't. What would you do if a giant meteor hit the earth in eight hours and you knew you were going to die? And the answer is: Nothing! You'd carry on as usual, watching the meteor grow in the sky while you did the dishes.

After the class I go down to Starbuck's in the foyer and drink a latte as I watch the students swarming to and fro as they try to find the room for their next class. My friend from the conference stops in front of me. "Have you heard that Ronald is dead?" she asks without further introduction as she pushes her glasses back up on her nose.

"Yes."

"They say it was a heart attack but why are the forensics here, then?"

"I don't know."

"He was really unpopular with some of the Nazis," she says and smiles. We've previously discussed the preoccupation with Nazism at the Department which we've both become sick and tired of.

"So it seems." I consider whether I should say anything about how he died but there doesn't really seem to be any reason for that, besides, she'll beat me to the punch, anyway.

"I've gotta go," she says. "I'm going up to hear about doctors from hell, but I'll probably see you later. Jenny has called a meeting tomorrow morning about what we're going to do now that Ronald's gone." She disappears up the stairs as I go back toward my office with the rest of my coffee in a plastic cup.

I meet several of my colleagues on my way back and in the hallway of the Department. They greet me but I feel that their attitudes change when they see me. It's as though the nature of their conversations change. I feel a little bit like when I as a big boy masturbated at my aunt's birthday and afterward I wasn't sure whether or not the other guests heard it through the bathroom door. That blend of uncertainty and inexplicable guilt feels the same way as now. It seems like my colleagues are looking at me as though they know something I don't. I greet Alison and Paulina who are discussing something in front of the couch where Tim as usual is sitting and reading. I don't get a chance to hear what they're talking about but I convince myself that I heard my name mentioned before they caught sight of me. I stop and would actually like to talk with them about Ronald but they make it clear I'm not welcome. Tim doesn't even look up from his papers as the two women demonstratively talk about post-colonial feminism. Dusty comes out of her office and I smile but she walks past me without so much as a trace of a smile. I mumble that I'd better get going but even that is entirely ignored by Alison and Paulina.

I take a few steps toward Gunther's door but it is closed which it only is when he isn't there so I go to my own office where I greet William with the glass eye and The Hitler-Mustache who is standing in front of my door and talking. And I feel their scrutinizing gaze on the back of my neck when I let myself in and sit down in front of the computer. I let my door stand ajar so that I can follow the conversation but they quickly fall silent and they part ways. "Aufwiedersehen," says William."

"Tschuss."

It would probably be very convenient for them all to nail me for the murder. Mostly, of course, from the guilty parties.

I receive an email from Gunther, he can't meet up after all and one from Jenny. Ronald died of a heart attack, she writes and she sends her warmest thoughts to his family and friends and all of us who have lost a warm-hearted and good colleague. She also calls an emergency meeting early tomorrow morning between nine and ten, just as my friend informed me. There will be no agenda, and it isn't timely but she asks for our understanding given the circumstances.

At that very moment someone knocks on the door. I look up and see Jenny. "May I have a brief word with you?" she asks and is already entering the office.

"Of course. I was just reading your email."

"How well did you know Ronald?" she asks and I sense there is more to the question than meets the eye. Firstly, because she never comes to my office to chit chat, secondly because there is something in her tone, the way in which she phrases her question.

"Not very well. I haven't been here for all that long

a time. But we talked quite a bit, drank beers together a couple of times, and I liked him."

"You were seen at the Department last night. What were you doing here?"

"Working overtime."

"Several heard you and Ronald arguing. Several think you may have had something to do with this."

"Didn't he die of a heart attack?" I feel a cold sensation spreading from the knot in my stomach.

She hesitates. "Yes, but they can be triggered." Then she changes her style. "I just thought you ought to know," she says. "Of course I don't think you had anything to do with it." She looks at me with her penetrating gaze. "Did you hear anything last night?" she then asks.

"I actually heard the door open a few times, but I thought it was the cleaning people. So I didn't give it much thought or look into it any further." Jenny is the last person I would confide in. I've tried getting entangled in accusations before in which she wasn't exactly supportive.

She gets up, nods curtly and leaves the office. "Remember, we have a meeting tomorrow, it's very important that you come."

I remain seated and stare into space for a while after she's left. Outside my door Hermann and William have shown up again and I can hear they are talking about deviations in the endings of verbs in Texan-German.

I really don't know what to do. There is no one here in whom I can confide and I don't know what I'd confide, anyway. I guess guilt is a rather subjective entity when it comes down to it. The possibility that my finger prints may be detected in Ronald's office, perhaps even next to his body, cannot be ruled out. That's going to be hard to explain now that I've claimed to have absolutely nothing to do with the case. The only thing I can do is try to find out who the murderer is on my own. Which already sounds like a cliché in itself. I lean back in my chair and look at the ceiling. So, how does one go about doing something like that? I've never been too crazy about who-dun-its and rarely read suspense novels. But isn't there something about dark alleyways, unexpected guests at the office, secret phone calls and a voice-over using the hero's inner monologue?

At least Emily's key gives me access to all the offices, so I guess I'll just have to start from one end and see what happens. And hope my shrewd and analytical conscience helps me some of the way.

An Abuse of Power

Imust have dozed off a little again because it is 5 pm when I find myself in my chair in front of my writing desk with my computer turned on. It's completely quiet here. I go out to the hallway and find that the couch is empty and the door to the main office is closed. I take a walk around and run into Alison who is busy packing up.

I go down and get a Coke from the soda machine on the ground floor and while the machine persistently spits out my crinkled bill, I check to make sure there are no basement steps next to it. There is actually a door but there is nothing but cleaning products behind it and I do recall seeing the Mexican ladies taking their cleaning things from there. I run into Alison on my way back up the stairs. She is carrying a light jacket over her arm and her genuine leather bag in her hand. There are sweat stains at the arm pits of her rose colored shirt and she is bent forward as she walks down the stairs. I nod to her but she looks straight through me.

I open the door to my own floor and let it slam shut behind me. I notice the light has been shut off in the reception and the clock that indicates when it will reopen is set to 9. I remain standing within the door opening and listen, but aside from the humming of the ventilator there isn't a sound. I go over to Gunther's office which is closed and then I walk down the hallways around the office island. There is literally no life to be found anywhere on this floor, everyone must have gone home, or wherever they usually go when they're not here: bars, swinger clubs, or hunting. What do I know? I consider whether I may have missed a notice for a meeting but Alison would most certainly have been there and not on her way down the steps with her sweat stains.

There is something impersonal and institutional about the closed veneer doors and the hallway toward which they are closed. The walls are kept in indecisive light colors you would never select for your home and the lighting is efficient but cold. There are a couple of places where there is a bulletin board with descriptions of courses that will be offered and short notices, a poster of a German village, a mountainous landscape and still photographs of *Metropolis* and *Teifland*.

I take out Emily's keys. What power. I can get into all the offices and I plan to abuse it in the most scandalous way. Perhaps that's why we don't have access to the A keys. I'll have to bring that up at the staff meetings. I look down the hallway. Where does one start? I think and listen in the darkness. A lonely detective in a dark labyrinth of hallways. Seen from a bird's eye view way up high.

I don't really have a primary suspect, so I start from the beginning, at the closest door, which so happens to be Paulina's. I try fitting several keys into the keyhole before finding the right one. For each failed attempt I listen out into the hallway and am considerably relieved when the fourth key manages to turn the cylinder. I've been in here once in connection with the case regarding my students' complaints. Paulina was very nice and she listened to me with an understanding smile and fluttering eyes as I stammered through my story, but she couldn't help me. She said some commonalities, wrapped in sensitive psycho-lingo. She is the employee representative and she must have taken some course in connection with that because she acted completely differently than she normally does. Her pauses weren't quite as prolonged and her empathy seemed genuine enough.

I basically don't do anything other than look around before leaving the office. She has maybe about seven books in her bookshelf and nothing in her drawers. She's probably the person who spends the least time at the Department. She has something so devious as a life outside her job and I have a hard time believing she contains enough evil to actually kill another colleague. But then again, I've been known for lacking judgment when it comes to people.

Taking turns, I let myself in to Dusty's, William's and Hermann's offices without finding anything. They furnish their offices very differently, some as an extended living room, others as an academic workshop, all of them have some trace of the Second World War on their shelves and in their instruction notes lying about, which, for example both Dusty and William have on their writing desks. They are not all entirely objective, I notice, but then again, who is? Hermann's office smells of pipe smoke but I doubt he smokes in there. Indoor smoking—as well as drinking—is considered equivalent to the likes of murder, pedophilia and rape, so the smell must come from his brown cardigan which is hanging over his writing desk chair, in his slippers under the table, or in the books he brought with him from home placed in a high book shelf. There are also pictures of his wife and three grown children.

For some reason or other I start from the bottom. Not that I have any primary suspects in mind, but I am somehow convinced that none of those four had anything to do with the matter. I was just beating around the bush.

Tim's office is the last one in the row. I listen once again at the door and this time I also knock because it wouldn't be unlike Tim to be working late. Time escapes him and then he's suddenly sitting there, having completely forgotten himself behind his pile of papers. Oftentimes he listens to bizarre music on the internet, German march music or Norwegian trance, and he has several times called me over with an almost childish enthusiasm to share his latest musical discovery. Right now there isn't a single sound, so I risk my neck and unlock the door. Tim would probably kill me if he knew I was about to rummage through his sanctuary without his knowledge or permission. Despite his constant mess he's a true control freak right down to his fingertips.

The office faces the park, but is located opposite Ronald's. The street lights from the parking lot cast a soft glow on the piles of papers. Some of them have piled up above his head and from the door it is impossible to see whether he is actually sitting at his writing desk. There are books and papers everywhere, on the floor, the writing desk, the chairs. There isn't a single spot where you can sit down or place a pencil. A fly buzzes around in confusion proving the rule.

Tim is of Irish descent. There is a small Irish flag on the windowsill and several books about Ireland on the bookshelf. There are also several colorful biographies about Irish people that shouldn't be on an academic's bookshelf, but Tim is way above what one should or shouldn't do. He puts them together ostentatiously and has probably never read them; he's more likely to have read Joyce, Yeats and Heaney, which there is room for, after all. Tim is way out of his depth, and there's something liberatingly haughty about his value relativism. When you know your own material as thoroughly as he does, it's wonderfully intimidating to encroach on other people's, and you can therefore never feel on safe ground with Tim. He always has an obscure yet relevant title he can throw into a discussion. And you are better able to understand it when you move through the numerous piles of newspaper clippings he has collected from all over the world.

I flip through a few pages here and there, but it's completely overwhelming: Child abuse, doping, sociology of literature, fan culture, Texas Germans, the Holocaust. Most of it is notes, clippings and articles from over twenty years of research and instruction. But it turns out that the piles have a system. At the bottom of a stack dealing with the persecution of the Jews, I find an archive box with a swastika. It contains a note with R.I.P. written on it, and underneath it are some faded pictures of men of different ages. Some are black and white photos from the War with some very serious looking young men wearing the uniform of the Wehrmacht, others in color, and in a few places I recognize a Texan landscape, Fredericksburg and San Antonio. In an envelope I also find a number of photos taken here at the university. Several of them feature some of the professors from the Department, as well as the dean and the blonde lady I saw in Jenny's office. For some reason, there are more of Alison: Alison in an academic outfit, Alison at the bottom of the tower in an A-line summer dress, Alison heiling at the photographer in front of the Department at dusk. Damn, I think to myself. It could be a joke, of course, but then why put it in a box of Nazi photos? In one way, it doesn't surprise me much, but in another, I shudder to see it so manifest, the symbol of evil unfolded just below the window here by a colleague who I may not have the greatest veneration for, but have nonetheless spoken to several times.

I put the photos back in the box and place it at the bottom of the stack, placing the piles of paper on top. I make sure everything looks the same as when I arrived. Then I leave the office.

Untimely Fascination

I skip Ronald's office, which is still sealed off with police tape, and head to Alison's. Several clues point to her, so why waste more time rummaging through other people's drawers? I must be feeling the heat too, because I feel a tingle in my stomach as I open the door to her office. Besides, I've never actually been in here before. I haven't been invited, and it has never occurred to me to visit her on my own. Until now.

The office is surprisingly cozy. Or maybe it's not so surprising. She's basically moved her life in here, complete with a coffee maker, a fridge and a small television. She sits in here and chills out, and now that I see it, I remember one of the Mexican cleaners complaining about her once. There were limits to what they would put up with, even as illegal laborers, and Alison was apparently the limit. There are leftover chips and cookie crumbs on the floor, and some raisins have gotten stuck in the carpet under the chair, but it doesn't seem disgusting. There's also a fresh smell and the desk is tidy, with only two stacks of papers and a couple of pens. On the bookshelf, the books are in alphabetical order, no fiction, but monographs on post-feminism, cyber-feminism and third wave feminism, World War II, Jewish studies and revisionism. Under H is an immaculate copy of *Mein Kampf*, *Hitler's Secret Conversations 1941-1944* and *Hitler's Secret Book*, as well as a number of biographies; *The Last Days of Hitler*, *Who Voted for Hitler?* and *Hitler: Diagnosis of a Destructive Prophet*. It could be the collection of a keen scholar, but it undeniably gives a different perspective when you've just seen her heil. When does interest peak, when does academic probity turn into untimely fascination? There is already something perverted about dealing so thoroughly with ... something.

I look behind the books on the bookshelf and pull out the desk drawers, but find nothing. An unopened pack of Fig Newtons and a toothbrush, some clips and a stack of business cards: Dr. Alison Fuchs, Ph.D. I turn on her computer, but of course it's password-protected, and I try the most obvious ones I can think of, but fail because I don't know her very well. I don't know the name of her cat, which is on the shelf in a silver frame, her mother or favorite actor, and Hitler isn't it. They say that the vast majority of passwords refer to family members, pets, birthdays and the like, but I don't even know where she lives. I turn the computer back off.

I sit down in her office chair and turn halfway around so I can see her bookshelf. I pretend to be her. Isn't that how you do it? I remember how she's been acting the last few days, how she freaked out in the copy room, how she's been whispering with several of her colleagues, how she reprimanded Jenny. No doubt there's something fishy about her, but where would she hide the damning evidence? In a Hitler biography whose spine sticks out slightly from the others? It's either been glued up or it's been taken off. The rest of the books are in a straight line, so I pull it out, open it and find a small red leather notebook inside. The book is hollow, and I assume Alison herself has cut out the middle of the pages and glued the rest together.

It is written in neat handwriting and contains dated diary entries from a paranoid everyday life at university. I flip through the densely written pages, but then sit down at the desk and read the entries: "Hermann once again gave me a superior look across the conference room." "William spoke unfavorably about Jenny, he thinks she can be 'pushy' (in connection with job interviews)."

"Ronald has slept with Sigrun, she told me this evening after smoking more than usual. I pretended to go along with it, but didn't inhale." "Kristian is harmless, he's simply too naive to read the game." A month ago, she wrote a long passage about Ronald, who she clearly doesn't have much regard for. He has blackmailed his way into the Department, is "academically dishonest, lazy, alcoholic, condescending." He apparently has had something on several people and uses his old research results as a means of blackmail: "Now he threatens to publish his knowledge, and he will drag some of the old ones down with him. Including me? Paulina told me that he is writing a novel that will reveal everything." A little further on: "He doesn't seem to care about the consequences, nothing means anything to him anymore, including old promises."

I don't know how credible Alison's notes are, but I've heard several times now that Ronald has had his hands on various people. And that I myself am naive must be true.

If no one else at the Department was interested in the Second World War, I could stop my research here, but they are. That is the real tragedy. If only there had been a hole where *Mein Kampf* should have been, but here it is, in a perfectly fine edition with a stiff binding and gold lettering. Next to it are a number of videos, German war classics, and I remember the scene in the copy room again: "Touch these and die," I think. Maybe that's just what Ronald did. I get up, lock myself out of Alison's office, walk to the main office. I can hear a door slam on the floor below me, but there's still no sound up here. I lock myself into the reception area and close the door gently behind me. I don't bother locking it. In case anyone surprises me, I can say the door was open and I wanted to check if anything was wrong.

I find Alison's videos in a corner. Stacked together on one of the shelves with a note on top that simply reads: "Belongs to Alison." She must have picked them back up off the floor and off the shelves after I left. I find a bag from the academic bookstore and put them in it before heading out to the reception. I look around now that I'm here and quickly find Emily's women's magazines in a cabinet in the desk drawer, a Ricky Martin fan magazine, nail polish, makeup, a pink manicure set and some dieting powder. She didn't stick deeper than that. The door to Jenny's office is open, but I feel pretty sure I wouldn't find anything in there. The office is too public for her to hide anything. The door is always open and the secretaries go in and out, even when she's not there. I stand in the doorway for a while and look around, but give up and instead leave the main office, lock the door behind me and walk to the AV room, which is opposite the reception.

As I'm about to unlock the door, I hear footsteps on the stairs outside and I hurry to unlock it, slip inside and lock the door behind me. My heart is pounding. I can hear someone entering the floor, the front door slamming but no voices, a pair of sneakers whose rubber soles squeak against the floor. I can't tell if it's a man or a woman.

I don't dare turn on the lights in the room, but I know I am very familiar with it. This is where we keep audio tapes for classes, large tape recorders and various electronic equipment. I can feel some of it right in front of me, and I carefully sit down against the wall just inside the door so as not to knock anything over. I sit like this for a long time. Finally, after thinking things through, I muster up enough courage to take off my polo shirt.

I roll it up and place it under the door to insulate it, so I can turn on a light without risking anything leaking out. In the light, I set up a TV and a pair of headphones. I load the first video into the machine, turn the screen away from the door and turn the lights back off. I make sure you can't hear the sound outside the headphones before I put them on and stand against the wall to the left of the TV. The room is microscopic, yet there is room for three televisions, as well as the large tape recorders and several boxes of tapes and wires and electronic gadgets.

It's very claustrophobic to shut out the world under such circumstances, to sit with headphones when I know being in this room goes against the rules and that an unidentified person is lurking outside the door. It seems as if the walls are so thin you can hear me breathing or the gentle crackle of the worn tape before the movie starts.

Greetings from Buchenwald

It is a terrible performance I have invited myself to. I've fast-forwarded a lot while watching five tapes, but I managed to get the essence, and now I'm left with a bad case of nausea as I sit in the dark. I have turned off the TV, put my headphones on and sat against the wall next to the door to digest the impressions

The tapes are homemade. Alison must have been busy at the editing table. They may not be cut very well, but the result is effective and the music track covers up the worst cuts in the audio.

The first tape shows a handful of my colleagues at a meeting. It could be innocent, but it begins with a red swastika and a greeting with their right arms raised. I recognize several of my colleagues: Alison, Sigrun and Dusty, but there are a few others the camera didn't manage to capture. I can see the others sometimes look at them and say something. The sound is very poor. Occasionally there are clips from old war movies, from Riefenstahl's Olympics, from a speech with the Führer, to illustrate important points from the meeting. I guess. They don't seem to have any hidden agendas, but talk about the story as if it were their own. At one point, Tim talks passionately about the early attempts at doping in the run-up to the Olympics, about the important medical results obtained from experiments on prisoners of war. This is illustrated with clips from Buchenwald and the nodding of his colleagues.

The next few tapes are in the same style, but on one of them there is some recent footage that makes my stomach turn. It appears to be an interrogation for academic misconduct, but the accused has a sack over his head and is sitting naked on a chair. A fit young guy of foreign ethnicity. He stutters and cries, but his arms are pulled further back whenever he answers incorrectly.

The last tape is with Ronald. They must have been watching him for a long time. It's a kind of video diary, and the date of each episode is embossed on the bottom of the screen. You hear him making calls from the office, you see him leaving the Department, talking to me in the hallway or sitting behind the computer writing and drinking. There are no actual revelations, but it almost has to mean that whoever they are, they have a sequence with the murder on another tape.

I'm about to pull the last tape out of the video when

I'm interrupted by the returning footsteps. I freeze with my hand out. The same squeaky rubber soles. I can hear a door closing and then the approaching footsteps. Like an echo of a dream.

A little while later I hear them pass by and then, to my surprise, some muffled voices a little further down the hall. One is Tim's, I'm almost sure I recognize his slightly self-important, nasally voice. The other is a woman's. I remove my polo shirt from the door and lie down with my eye as close to the crack under the door as I can get. It's enough for me to see a pair of white tennis shoes that must belong to Tim and a pair of red pumps. How she snuck in here wearing those without my discovering it I can't fathom. I can see the bottom of a pair of older women's legs that I don't immediately recognize. They are well-groomed and don't look like scholarly legs. I strain to make out what they are talking about. At first it's just generalities, but then I catch my name, "but who is this Himmelstrup?" she asks and Tim replies something about me being perfect for the job, that I have a special ability to always be in the wrong place at the right time, and then they both laugh. Tim's feet tilt up and down when he speaks, I've never noticed that before, hers are completely still. They are about to say something more, but then the front door opens and I can hear a voice say "Thanks for a nice evening." "Yes, thank you for a nice evening" Tim and the woman reply in unison before leaving the floor together. Tim first, I can just see the white tennis shoes stop at the door to hold it, while her red pumps trip out.

My heart is pounding and my throat is dry. For many years, I felt like this when I had to speak in large gatherings, but these days it takes more than that. Since the world lost its colors, I haven't had palpitations, so it's nice to try it again. To feel alive and that something matters. I look out through the crack under the door again and see a pair of black shoes approaching. Then I hear a bunch of keys rattling, a key turning in the cylinder above my head and the door opening. I look up. "You don't have to hide anymore," says a voice which I instantly recognize.

Hermann Hartmann

The light falls obliquely on him from the outside, dividing his face into shadows of light and darkness. It's Hermann. Half of his Hitler moustache is visible, as is the shadow of his leather cap. "I thought you might come back," he says, reaching his hand down towards me so I can stand up. Otherwise, he ignores the fact that I'm lying topless in a darkened AV room bending down at the opening of the door. He's a gentleman to the bone.

"Was it good for you too?" I try as I stand up and put on my shirt. He ignores that.

"You're on the right track," he says instead, "but you have no idea what you're getting yourself into. Do you?"

"No." I shake my head. "I just don't want to be lynched for something I didn't do."

One corner of his mouth pulls up into something resembling a smile. "No, that wouldn't be very pleasant, either," he says, and must notice my concern, because he continues: "Don't be afraid, I'm here to help you. There's something I want to show you. Ronald spoke highly of you and trusted you, so I do too. You were even set to star in his mystery novel, which he finally got around to writing when you arrived."

"I know."

"You had it in you, he thought, you'd make a good character in a novel." He pushes me out of the small room and heads down the hallway. "Sorry," he says, "but you're not the best person to be seen with right now."

"I can imagine."

We walk down the hallway in silence. Hermann is clearly on guard. He listens for eavesdroppers and looks around before continuing in a hushed voice. "Ronald has been studying creative writing for many years, but never came up with a workable template for his novel. He had big plans for it, things had to come to light, and this Department had to be put on display. When he saw your foreign eyes, it all came together. You know, you can only see your own position from the outside."

"I thought he was nice. I thought he was genuinely interested in my stories." Hermann nods. "Recently he read *Confessions of a Novelist* by the Russian linguist and critic Igor Browatski, I don't know if you are familiar with it? He was very interested in it, and it cleared the last obstacles out of the way. And then you came along. If you knew what notes he had. But that's one of the things I want to show you."

"Why?"

"Don't ask so many questions! Just play along! You don't have too many better alternatives right now."

"I guess you have a point". Hermann rarely uses forceful expressions, so that alone tells you something about his state of mind. So does his posture. It's not as casually upright as it used to be. He walks slightly hunched over and it's clear he's on guard.

He turns the corner, looks both ways and then waits for me to follow. He nods in acknowledgment. He has always been very gallant. He's the type who pulls out his chair when a lady sitting near to him needs to use the restroom, and I've seen him several times running to open the car door for his wife when he parks his modest Geo outside the Department. He lives half an hour south of the city in a small village with a German-sounding name. Still, he can be brusque and is known for saying things directly and bluntly. I've been reprimanded several times when I've mispronounced some German verbs or arrived late for one of the teachers' meetings. Tough but fair, isn't it?

He shows me his palm and then brings an index

finger up to his mouth. Wait and be quiet, I decipher. I stop. He looks around the next corner and beckons me over. It's all very proper, almost militaristic, and I'm not surprised. I'm sure he's been both a scout leader and an officer. The erect posture, the effective hand signals, the well-trimmed mustache. He disappears around the corner, but reappears shortly afterwards and waves me along. Then he opens the door opposite Tim's office and together we step into a small room that must be right in the central axis of the building. He closes the door behind us, flips on a switch and resumes his story in a hushed voice.

"I met Ronald at Concordia College of Selma, Alabama, where he was a music appreciation instructor. I was only a couple of years younger than him, and he was also the only white teacher at the school. And I was the only white student at the time, so it was kind of natural for us to spot each other." He looks over his shoulder before elaborating. "It's traditionally a black college, founded by the Lutheran Church in the 1920s to improve the cultural and spiritual condition of the blacks," he explains. He has made his way through the office and is now moving a desk that is blocking a door on the opposite side. He approaches things with a matter-of-factness hard to put into words. After moving the desk, he takes a key out of his pocket and unlocks the door. "Here you go," he says, gesturing into darkness. "Unfortunately, there's no light up here, but there's a handrail and the stairs are easy to walk on in the dark. It's not slippery and the steps are even". He remains standing with his hand invitingly in the air until I enter the stairs first. "Go down a few steps so I can come in," he says kindly. Then he follows and closes the door behind us. It's impossible to see a hand in front of you, so I stand still until he has entered. "Do you still want me to lead the way?" he asks, overhauling me on the stairs before I can answer. "You can hold on to my shirt."

Once we've descended a few steps, he continues his story. He speaks in a normal tone of voice now. Maybe even a little louder than usual, so I don't miss any of the details. "So, we found each other and started meeting after school at a coffee shop, I think it was called Southern Hub. At first we discussed literature and music, but we also started going to the theater, readings and exhibitions. And then we started sleeping with each other." He hesitates before taking the next step down the endless staircase. Even though you couldn't hear it in his voice, it still cost him a little to admit it. "When rumors started to spread, he found another job. In any case, it didn't look good that the only two white people in the entire university spent so much time together and did nothing to integrate with the rest of the school.

"Ronald wasn't a very good teacher, but he tried, which is why the students were quite fond of him. He had a built-in sensibility that we liked. But he moved on and was hired at Gustavus Adolphus College as a teaching assistant. We stayed in touch, and I was instrumental in getting him into the university." We're finally on solid ground again. Hermann walks over and turns on the light switch, which makes me squint. He walks across a small hallway, opens a door opposite the stairs and goes inside. I follow him. He flips another switch, but it takes a few seconds for the fluorescent tubes to react, blinking noisily and finally throwing a flickering light down towards us.

Sugar Cubes and Powdered Milk

I was expecting the room to look like the one in the dream, but it doesn't at all. For one thing, Hitler isn't here. On the other hand, there are books and boxes in file cabinets all along the walls. They are also standing out in the middle of the room, so it's impossible to get an overview of their size. I try to look down one row, but I can't see the end. "It takes up the entire floor plan," says Hermann.

"What's in all the boxes?"

"We'll get to that in a moment."

Hermann has positioned himself a little inside the door, upright, with one hand resting on the waistband of his pants and the other stroking his moustache. He looks as if he is starting to regret the situation. Maybe I'm wrong, because he smiles at me and opens his arms out towards the room.

"Like so many others around here, Ronald became obsessed with the Second World War. He started by reading all the classics about the War, theoretical masterpieces and literary milestones, but gradually his empathy grew beyond the books. He wanted to create his own history, to elaborate on it, to get it under his fingernails, to merge with it. He decided to expose the War criminals. I remember we had a late-night conversation when he was employed at St. Olaf, where he had just decided to dedicate his life to that cause. I don't think it was really because of moral considerations, but he thought it was a good story and something that could provide a sense of meaning to an otherwise empty existence. I had just gotten a job here at the university and had the impression that it would be a good place from which to work. It's no secret there are many Germans in Texas who don't exactly have a clean slate."

I've walked over to one of the shelves and am looking at the archive boxes, all of which have yellow labels with intricate numbers on them. "Don't you want a cup of coffee?" Hermann suddenly asks. "I haven't had any coffee at all today, and I won't be able to tell you more if I don't have some. I can quickly make a pot." He points to a kitchenette in the far corner. I nod and follow him there. "I gave him some names and ideas of who he might want to look into more closely, and he went to work on that. He buried himself in history, and during a research semester in Germany, he gained access to a classified section of the Berlin State Archives, where he collected a lot of useful material on high-ranking professors at this university. They may not have fought for the Fatherland themselves, but their fathers had either been high-ranking officers or responsible for melting gold teeth into gold bars in Buchenwald." Hermann pauses as he empties the coffee filter of stale coffee, pours water into the machine and starts it up. He bends down and opens one of the cupboards under the coffee machine. "I think we even have some powdered milk and sugar. As far as I remember, you use milk, right?"

"Yes."

Hermann rummages around inside the cupboard and comes out with a small glass bowl with sugar cubes, powdered milk and small colored straws for stirring.

"So he blackmailed his way into university?"

"In a way, yes. You could say that. I put his name forward when a position opened up, and of course I helped him get the position. It was never said directly what would happen if he didn't get the job. But we talked about his great interest, his research results and what his future research would be about. Just like you do in a job interview. Of course, he tailored the research area depending on who he was talking to. He had a hold on almost all the old-timers at the Department, and he played his cards perfectly. There was no doubt when it came to vote for the candidates."

"Who did he find something on?"

"Most of them, but you'll have to find out for yourself," says Hermann, pointing to the archive. "It's all here. It's cataloged and easy to access if you know the system. I don't, he never gave me the key to this labyrinth, and there's enough reading material here for seven or eight hundred FTEs, I guess. And where do you find so many trusted employees these days?" Hermann looks at me questioningly and I raise my shoulders in response. He turns to the coffee machine, which has started to make slurping sounds indicating that it's about to finish. He waits until it stops dripping, takes the pot out of the machine and pours coffee into two identical cups. He hands one of them to me and points to a small table. There's a chair with some papers on it, which he removes before retrieving another stool from behind a bookcase.

"Here you go," he says and sits down on the

stool. I pick up the powdered milk before I sit down, sprinkle a packet in the coffee and watch it settle on top of it before it slowly begins to sink. I use the plastic straw to stir it, giving me something to do. We sit like this for a while without saying anything. I turn the coffee cup in my hand as I look around the room. Hermann seems to have sunk into himself. "What did he do after he was hired? Did he continue fundraising or had he achieved what he wanted?"

"That's a good question," Hermann nods. He pauses for a moment in thought before continuing. "He kept going for a while, but lost the spark. He didn't really see the point, now that he had utilized the data he had collected. What was the point if he couldn't use the results for his own gain? He half-heartedly published a few articles, but he had mostly seen it as a game, a strategic game. He liked chess a lot."

"I played with him once. He won big time."

"Mmm. He tried to cultivate new interests and areas of research. Shortly after he was hired, he set up a listening station and began monitoring everything and everyone, including himself. He taped radio and TV broadcasts, phone conversations and internet chats. He cut out articles from the newspaper and downloaded things from the internet. He collected gigabytes of material, shelves of articles and transcripts miles long. But gradually he began to lose his ability to distinguish fact from fiction. He was living in a dream world, and his novel became an obsession. It entered reality, and what he wrote flowed in his consciousness with what he experienced. And he wrote everything down: dreams, thoughts, ideas, teacher's notes. Those boxes over there, for example, contain short summaries of all the books he's read," he says, pointing to a shelf some distance away. I look over there.

"Oh my God."

"Yes. Ronald was very concerned about what would happen after he was gone. He wanted to be sure to leave something lasting and to pass on his experience."

"Did he have any children? I've heard so many different stories that I have no idea what's true. He never told me anything himself, but I don't have the impression that he had any social relationships other than his dogs."

"They actually live with me now, but my wife is not enthusiastic about having them, so I don't know what's going to happen to them. I've tried to explain to her they are more than dogs and that we owe it to Ronald to take care of them. But she thinks they're messy and smelly and badly behaved." Hermann takes a sip of his coffee and smoothes out his mustache with the inside of his index finger.

"But did he have any family besides the dogs?" I ask again.

Hermann stands up and disappears between the rows. I can hear him pulling out some boxes as he talks to himself. Then he comes back with a black box of pictures, which he places on the table between us.

"I remembered where that one was," he says happily, "otherwise, as I said, it's almost impossible to find anything in here."

He flips through the pictures and I look on with curiosity. "For a while, he tried to take pictures of everyone he met. Later, he switched to only taking pictures of those he slept with or who meant something to him. That alone became a nice collection." I remember he almost always had a small camera with him and he also took several pictures of me. He asked the waiter at the bar where we had a beer a while back to take a picture of both of us, and he took one of me one of the first times I visited him in his office. He did it in a way that made you feel a little bit chosen.

"Would you like more coffee?" Hermann asks and stands up.

"No, thank you."

I flip through the photos while Hermann goes to get more coffee. In one of them, a young girl is standing under a tree in the park outside our building. She is clearly a student. She's wearing plaid socks, a short pleated skirt and a slightly oversized T-shirt. She smiles flirtatiously. The sky is blue with a single small cloud hovering over the stadium further behind.

"There's no telling if he slept with her," says Hermann, who has returned carrying his coffee in his hand and is now standing behind my chair. I didn't hear him at all.

"That's the magic of the pictures. That they hold memories for the person who took them, but for the rest of us, they open a lot of possibilities for interpretation. Did the old professor really fuck the cute young student, or had he already done it? If so, what had he promised her in return? Or was he just helping her with an essay under the tree in the park on a sunny fall day?"

Hermann sits back down on the stool. "As you can see, he met a lot of people. Some of the photos he showed me himself. There was one in particular that he was a little proud of. Otherwise, he rarely boasted about his conquests, but this one," Hermann says, rummaging through the box, "he showed me once when we were down here together."

He hands me a picture in a small plastic pocket. It shows a girl lying on her stomach on an orange sofa. The camera is zoomed in on her bottom. It looks soft.

"That's Angelina's bottom," Hermann says, laughing. "Angelina Jolie's. She visited the university once in the early 90s and Ronald showed her around. She never started studying here, but Ronald got what he wanted out of the situation. He was quite proud of that picture."

Hermann absentmindedly flips through the box. "I know several of the people in the pictures. I've taught several of them myself, which is why Ronald kept a low profile with his conquests. But you asked if he had any family? Actually, he didn't. He had a girlfriend for a few years and they had a son together, but Ronald couldn't settle down. There were too many girls—and men—he wanted to get to know better."

Hermann studies a few photos before dropping them back into the box. He looks up at me.

"Did he ever see his son?"

"He and his girlfriend split up when his son was quite young and they lost contact. But I know that Ronald himself went to see him when he turned 16. He gave him a car and an apology and I think they saw each other a bit after that. He didn't tell me about it, but I know he entrusted him with the key to a listening station I don't even know where is. The son is not the sharpest tool in the box, so what he gets out of it, God knows."

Distracting Cartoons

Hermann takes a sip of his coffee and it's as if the mood in the room changes. As if the light is dimmed slightly, the color of the walls takes on a greenish hue and the shadows are blurred. "Ronald told me he had also found something about me, and of course I'm excited to read about that. I also know somewhere along the line he identifies his killer. He had planned the end of his book and calculated all the probabilities. Nothing could take him or his fiction by surprise anymore, he claimed."

He stands up and signals for me to follow. We walk down the aisle between the shelves where the archive materialis standing in piles.

"What have you found out?"

"Not a thing, to be honest. I can't figure out the system and I'm already bogged down in meaningless printouts, recipes, minutes and notes. I don't have the patience for that kind of stuff. But then I remembered he once told me he had given you the key. Indirectly. So now I'd like you to help me find the solution to all this. It must be in both of our interests." I look at him in surprise.

"He never mentioned the room to me, and I had no idea he was doing anything like this in his spare time. I hardly knew him at all. We just had a few beers together and I thought he was a nice guy."

"Have you slept with him?"

I can't help but feel a little offended. Having sex with a man of retirement-age is not part of my self-image and I was hoping it would show.

"No."

"Well, you've meant a lot to him. You're the main character in his novel, and he talked about you a lot. Don't you remember him telling you something about a code, a number system, a key to a secret?"

I think about it for a moment.

"You're hesitating," Hermann says sharply.

"I'm trying to think, but I really can't remember anything like that. We mostly talked about literature and music when we met. A few times about teaching and his problems with the students."

"I think we should try something anyway," says Hermann, pointing to a door at the side of the room. "Maybe you've just forgotten."

I follow Hermann into a small room. He turns on

the light switch inside the door to the right. As in the archive room outside, there are no windows, but there are no books, boxes or loose papers either. There is a small desk with a computer, desk lamp and a printer along one wall and a low bookcase along the other. In the middle of the floor is a glass table with wheels on a patterned pink fringed rug. Next to the desk is a wooden chair with wooden armrests, and in front of the desk is a high-backed office chair with blue upholstery. Hermann rolls out the office chair and sits down. He points to the other chair and says "Please." I sit down.

On the walls are pictures of dogs of different ages, a puppy with overly large paws, a hunting dog with shiny fur and a pheasant in its mouth and an emaciated, old German Shepherd. There is a bulletin board upon which pictures hang with colored pins, as well as a few comic strips clumsily cut out from various newspapers. Comic strips are always abused in research environments. They are pasted on doors and walls in offices, meeting rooms and kitchens to signal humanity and to demonstrate that even smart people have a sense of humor. We're not that dry, they are saying, and we understand perfectly well how young people communicate. The favorite ones are typically by Gary Larson and Bill Watterson, and it's one of Larson's hanging on this bulletin board, something about a conductor being let into a room full of happy banjo players in Hell.

While I've been looking around, Hermann has been busy rummaging through a desk drawer, closed it and is now standing next to me, tying my arms to the armrests. I don't have time to react before it's too late and my arms are completely tied down to the chair. Just to be on the safe side, he also ties my legs to the chair legs. So that's how comic strips work too, as an excellent source of distraction for closet sadists to use on their victims.

"What are you doing?" I ask in a composed manner.

"I want to find out how much you really know. You don't have to be afraid. I'm tying you up for your own safety. So you don't get hurt when I give you the injection. You might get some spasms, but it shouldn't cause any long-term discomfort."

"I'm not sure I want to do that."

"No, you can't be expected to want to do everything. But it would be a great help, and I understood from you that you wanted to help. We just need to find out what you know."

He turns on the desk lamp and shines it at me. Then he walks to the door and turns off the ceiling light. The light from the desk lamp falls on him obliquely, distorting his face as he steps back, his eyes shining, and the shadow from his leather cap falls sharply across his forehead. He picks up something from the desk that I can't see before he steps halfway back into the light: A syringe. He pushes the needle into a small bottle with a rubber cap and pulls back the plunger. Then he pulls the needle out, adjusts the contents and taps the needle. He has to fiddle with my sleeve before he gets it rolled up, but manages to tie the rubber hose around my upper arm without much trouble. I look at him apathetically. I've always hated needles, but there's not much I can do. He taps a vein on my forearm before passing the tip of the needle through my skin and injecting its contents.

The Narration

It won't be long before I'm telling you everything. About my childhood on an abandoned farm somewhere in Jutland, snowball fights and soapbox derbies in the schoolyard at the village school. My car was number 13, I confide in him, and I won a flashlight for an honorable second place along with the shoe shop owner's son. I tell him about my childhood sweetheart and lunch packs with raspberry shortcakes in the forest. I spend time on the latter in particular, it must have made an impression, the sounds of the forest and the soft moss. My mother would never dream of giving me cake in my lunch pack, but Solvej, my girlfriend's mother, could. Hermann tries to get me to tell him about Ronald, but I feel it's important to include the background story. My first Christmas Eve alone in Zimbabwe, in front of the fireplace in a hostel, the apartments in Copenhagen, my studies, travels, my persistent girlfriend. My relationship with my family, my grandfather, who lives in a beautiful house in Copenhagen and steers the family with a hard hand, my father, whose taste in art I don't understand. And finally, I get to the trip to Texas. Hermann looks up with interest and takes out a pad and a pen.

"I arrived at Houston airport," I say and get stuck for a moment. "It took a long time to get through and there were several times when felt I had been harassed." I hesitate. The words no longer come to me naturally. "And then there was something about a girl called Angelina, some underground tunnels in a motel and flying over Texas."

Hermann smiles. "That's something you've read, isn't it?" he asks. "Try to concentrate. What happened next? When did you arrive at the university? How did you first meet Ronald?"

I try to think. Bits and pieces of memories run through my mind like a film, hazy black and white images.

"I was thrown into a dark room, tied down hand and foot. There was some water dripping far away in the distance, and the sound of little feet pitter pattering close by, and Philip, Philip, he's gone," I say as I tug at the cords holding me to the chair. As the realization dawns on me, I bow my head and break down in tears.

Hermann stirs nervously. It must have been hours, and now he seems to be losing his grip on the session. He gets up and walks out. He closes the door behind him and I sit alone in the small interrogation room for a while. I sit and talk quietly to myself, I can't keep my thoughts still, but I have to tell my story. And with every word that leaves my mouth, another layer is added to the construction that stands and wavers before my inner eye. Chronology and logic have long since given way to mental association, and each side story closes off other possible narratives and thereby opens up new ones. And it's all true. It's all my story, I think.

It's a while before I hear the door open. Apart from the sound of my own voice, it has been completely silent, but now Hermann is filling the room with his footsteps and then his voice. "Can I read something to you?" he asks kindly. "Something from Ronald's novel?"

"Of course," I reply.

"I found it in a box of notes and I think you'll find it interesting." He clears his throat before beginning to read: "In a flash I see myself raising *Mein Kampf* high above my head on the floor a few meters in front of me. I close my eyes and try to control my breathing. This is madness. Why would I kill Ronald, I think, looking down at my shaking hands. Why would anyone?'"

Ronald looks up at me with a smile.

"Coupled with this note: 'Kristian may be the killer, but he doesn't know it himself'."

"But it's a novel," I protest. "It's unreliable by definition, it's imagination, fantasy, fiction. The truth in cloaks."

"Exactly," says Hermann. He's no longer smiling.

What Happened Afterward

I can't remember what happened next, but when I come back to myself, Hermann is untying me. He looks satisfied.

"So," he says, "that wasn't so bad."

"What did you find out?" I ask, a little dazed. I rub my wrists like they do in the movies. Slowly and thoughtfully.

"A little bit of everything. That you know more than you think. And that you want to help."

"Well?"

"You're the key. So if I let you snoop around in the archive, I'm sure you'll find something. I'll let you do that. Unfortunately, I have some errands to run, so I have to go, but I'll come tomorrow and check on you." Hermann turns and walks towards the door to the archive. Before he reaches it, he turns as if he wants to say something, hesitates, looks at me for a moment, then changes his mind and goes into the archive. A moment later, I hear him open the door to the stairs and lock it behind him, his footsteps receding up the stairs. I sit back in silence and stare out into the air. A key, I think.

I'm the key to the archive? It doesn't make any sense.

I get up and go to the archive. It's cold, something I haven't noticed before. I'm wearing linen pants and a beige polo shirt. It seemed suitable to wear above ground, but down here it's not enough. The lighting here is also sparse. The fluorescent tubes only illuminate the area around the entrance, while the corridors dissolve into darkness further down. It's impossible to see the end of the rows of filing cabinets. They are spaced one meter apart all the way down through the room and are full of boxes, books, papers and folders. It smells like an archive and a basement, damp and dusty with piles of papers, and my chest is already tightening. My head is getting heavier than it already is, and I occasionally have to stop and support myself against the bookcase, bending my head down to meet the stars before my eyes.

Each shelf has a slip of paper with two letters and a multi-digit number, PA3787 in this case. There seems to be some numerical system, but it doesn't make sense if you don't know the system. I open some of the boxes and skim through old papers, but as Hermann said, it's all one big confusion and the notes don't make sense if you don't know what they are referring to.

I go and make a cup of coffee while I think things over, pouring powdered milk and sugar into the plastic cup and stirring with the useless teaspoon that looks like a straw. I find a pack of soft biscuits in a cupboard and sit down at the table where I sat with Hermann a few hours ago. The pictures are still there, some of them spread on the table, the rest carelessly thrown into the box. As I sit, I spot a brown cardigan hanging at the end of a row of shelves, and I get up and go and put it on. It smells of dust and old books.

Systematization and Knowledge-Based Organization

I decide to take a systematic approach. I get out a pencil and paper and start sketching the room before I begin to measure it out. It turns out to be about 70 meters long and 30 meters wide. There are 60 book cases that stand across the room. They are each 28 meters long, and they discontinue approximately one meter before each outer wall and are intersected by a central aisle so you can easily move down the axis of the room. It's very efficient and user-friendly, it is knowledge-based organization at an advanced level. Now I just need to figure out what that knowledge is and how it's organized.

I start from one end, open the box closest to the table, and find a stack of yellowed papers with names, short biographies and references to other numbers in the archive. I test one of the references, walk down the rows of shelves and find the number, MV5467. "Paul Pfarr," I mutter aloud, "Paul Pfarr," as my fingers search for the name. I pull out a sheet of paper listing his crimes, his current address in Williamsburg, his family and work history. His wife died several years ago, his sons are alive, one of them still lives in Williamsburg, another has moved to Houston, where he works as a beautician in a small company. None of them know about their father's past, but there is a reference to someone who does: PC2398. I flip through the yellowing papers in the box and find loose pieces of paper with Nazi quotes transcribed from radio and newspapers, the sources are at the bottom, carefully handwritten in small print. Albert Vögler's son lives in Williamsburg, where he runs a shop selling local specialties. Vögler was the head of Vereinigte Stahlwerke and was part of the secret meeting in 1933 where German big industry decided to pay for Hitler's election campaign. In 1978, Vögler Jr. married the then principal of a Catholic school in Houston. Together they had three children, none of whom know anything about their parents' past.

I follow a few more references and return to the point of departure where I open the box next to it. There are reading notes for various crime novels, plot summaries, characterizations, geographical observations, questions about the credibility of some of the information provided. There's a reference to Philip Kerr's *Berlin Noir* trilogy, and I go and get the box. I take it to the table, pick up a soft cookie and start flipping through the papers. I already know I'm too tired to find anything. I'd miss even the most obvious clue. So I give up, sit and stare into space as I suck on the cookie.

When I'm done with that, I take a walk around my cell to find a suitable place to sleep. I find a spot in the corner to the left of the entrance door, where I can lie somewhat concealed, but at the same time can keep an eye out if someone should enter. I fetch some archive boxes to shield myself from the draft, pull the bottom ones out of the shelf nearest the corner and distribute their contents underneath me, creating a sort of nest of information about War criminals and escaped Nazi sympathizers. I think of my bed at home, my wife and my warm duvet. Then I curl up, turn a couple of times, pull the cardigan over me and wait to fall asleep.

Hermann wakes me up a few hours later. He opens the door carefully and turns on the ceiling light, which I must have turned off. I look at the clock. It's half past six. Hermann looks around until he spots me. Then he smiles. "I apologize for coming so early," he says. 'But

I'm anxious to hear what you've found out'. I yawn and sit up, trying to remember where I am and what I should have found.

"Not much," I say. "I was just so tired I didn't get very far. I haven't found a system. Or the system is apparently that it's self-referential, and you can quickly get lost in the references."

"Yes, that's what I found, too." He sounds disappointed.

"I'll move on today," I hasten to add. I don't want to get up, because then he'll see the papers I'm lying on, and I don't know how he'll respond to that. That I'm desecrating the shrine, crumpling the records and sleeping on notes. Luckily, he walks over to the table. "Coffee?" he asks with a hint of German in his pronunciation. His English is otherwise impeccable. I nod, hurriedly gather the papers together and shove them into a file box as I stand up. I walk over to the table and take the same seat as yesterday, Hermann sits opposite me.

We drink coffee and talk about generalities, a bit about the faculty, my future plans, his relationship with Ronald, daily life above ground. Suddenly he puts his cup down a little too hard on the table, stands up and says goodbye. He turns at the door. "I'll check in again tonight," he says.

I follow him with my eyes. I drink the last of my coffee. I open the box from yesterday and place a small stack of papers on the table in front of me. They're about Kerr's trilogy. I take a sip of coffee and skim through the top papers. On one of them is a plot summary where all the plot points have been recorded in a diagram. He has graphically copied the novel according to his own system, reducing it to a two-dimensional drawing with obscure abbreviations. I stare, squint and focus on the drawing behind the notes. It's a plan of the library, I think. "It's a plan of the library," I say, turning towards the door that Hermann exited a moment ago.

THE NOVEL

Kerr's trilogy is set in 1936, 1938 and 1947, and Ronald has clearly adopted the idea of books as the cornerstone for building the archive. There are followers, war criminals and descendants, and they are divided into sections: MV, PC and GR, which stand for March Violets, The Pale Criminal and A German Requiem. It all makes sense. And I must be Bernhard Gunther in search of diamond necklaces, a low-ranking serial killer and dirty smugglers. The ending is up to me, wasn't it? I look at the page with the plot points. The lines intersect in several places and it's interesting to see the trilogy reduced—or elevated—to a single work. The references between the works are made clear, and the key, as Hermann has requested, is intertextuality. I jot down the points with the most intersecting lines and go to the archive.

In a box I find the first part of the novel along with some notes and computer printouts. The title page of the manuscript simply reads: "The Novel. Part One". It seems to be roughly the same one I read in his office the day before yesterday, but there are more notes and it's longer. I look at the clock. It's a little past 12. It would be nice if I could read it before Hermann returns.

I put the manuscript in front of me and turn to the first page with my right cheek resting against one hand. But then I still can't concentrate. I look out into the library. It's as if the darkness has closed in around me, and in the distance I can hear an eerie scratching sound. It could be a rat, I think, and try to focus my attention on the manuscript. So I arrive in Houston, meet Angelina and drive off in a Mustang. It's pretty close to reality and certainly to the version I've already read once. But just as I finally get the Mustang started, the rat really gets going, and now it's as if it's also got hold of a digging tool of some kind. At least I can hear more insistent digging sounds. Occasionally, they're close to knocking.

I stand up. The chair screeches across the floor, instantly making the sounds stop. I walk down the hallway, but there is nothing to see or hear. I don't know what I was expecting. The sounds are obviously not coming from in here, but still I bend down and look under a bookcase. I stay crouched down, completely still, for what feels like an eternity, before I give up and go back to my seat.

I've always been very good at studying for exams, so why not now? As long as I've had a deadline, I've always been able to keep my surroundings at bay. It's also been necessary, because I've never been good at keeping up during the year. But the exam is now, I think, when Hermann returns, and I'm already dreading the grade.

So: I arrive in Houston, meet Angelina and drive off in a Mustang. Then, gradually, come the conspiracy theories, Nazis, secret passageways and bizarre scholars. Ronald dies and the investigation begins. There are several footnotes in the text and several references to archive numbers. There's plenty to get to grips with here, and I note there are archive numbers for most of the employees at the Department. I must say, Ronald certainly was thorough when he did his preliminary research for his novel. There must be shelves several meters long containing the original source material upon which his characters are based. There seems to be more circumstantial evidence pointing to me, but Hermann can't be so certain, I sense, nor Tim or Alison. The woman with the blonde hair also appears in the text. She is a direct descendant of Hitler and has a stake in the story I can't make out. It ends at the most exciting point, but there is a reference to an archive number where the story may continue. I've just found Ronald's body and I hear voices in the hallway. I look up.

I must have really succeeded in shutting out my surrounding, because they have now returned with double strength. The scratching sounds have become considerably louder, and now are mixed with eager knocking noises. Not even a rat of considerable dimensions would be able to make such a noise. Occasionally, I think I also hear some muffled outbursts. I get up again and walk a few steps down the hallway, but then someone opens the door to the outside and the noise is immediately silenced.

A Well-Developed Sixth Sense

Hermann knocks on the open door and smiles at me. He doesn't say anything, but comes right up to the table and looks over my shoulder at the papers. He takes the booklet out of my hand and says something in German that I don't understand. Then he smiles and pats my hair, paternally.

"I knew I could count on you," he says. "Is everything here?"

"No, I was just about to look for the ending." I choose not to say anything about the notes. I can tell he's already satisfied, and I'd like to check the references first. Besides, there's no reason to point the finger at me as the killer yet. I have a feeling he'll take care of that himself.

"Then I won't disturb you," he says. "How did you come up with that?"

"The library is structured like Philip Kerr's *Berlin Noir* trilogy," I say. "Ronald often talked about the books, so in that way I knew the key. But I didn't figure it out myself, it was sort of random. I found his notes for the trilogy and behind them I could see the outline of the library."

"Of course it wasn't random. I don't believe in things being random, but 'reality can be arranged to resemble randomness', as Schreibner writes."

"Certainly." It is not wise to contradict Schreibner.

"Good work! Now I'll leave you alone so you can continue the search. I don't need to tell you I'm very excited about your results, do I? Why don't we say you'll tell me what you know tomorrow? Around ten o'clock." I have to nod, because he does, in response. Before he gets up and walks out he turns in the doorway and repeats: "Around ten o'clock."

The knocking sounds begin to intensify as soon as Hermann is out of the room. Whatever is knocking must be able to monitor the room or have a very well-developed sixth sense. I do a round in the archive, but still can't figure out exactly where it's coming from. But it's easier to localize the sound now. It's coming from somewhere behind the third shelf.

I haven't eaten anything other than soft cookies for a day and a half, and I can feel that I'm running out of energy. I'm entering a pleasantly drowsy state. I close my eyes and when I open them again, I think I see a dark blue figure floating between the shelves. My eyes close again and when I open them, it's gone. I pull Ronald's manuscript in front of me and this time I concentrate on the notes. I have to start almost from scratch to catch the first time my colleagues are mentioned. Gunther is the first, but of course there is no reference to him. He's too new, and aside from his weaknesses, I also feel I can delete him from the list of suspects. Emily has several numbers, and I choose to write them down on a piece of paper instead of going back and forth between the shelves and my desk.

Since I've gone through the entire manuscript, I have two pages of references in three columns. A list of names to the left and then the corresponding numbers in three rows. It's very systematic. I've done a good job. I say it out loud, "You've done a good job," I say it as if directed at someone else. As if I was someone else, an interlocutor, who needs a little encouragement. That's what solitude and reading does to you. You talk silently to the text, engage in dialog and need to get all the words you've absorbed, out. And then you don't realize you've crossed a line, that you're suddenly in the same category as bag ladies and vagabonds. "You've earned a little break," I say, nodding in agreement.

I spend the break scribbling faces on a piece of paper and thinking about nothing. Afterwards, I look for something edible in the cupboards with no luck, and for a toilet with better luck. I take a leak and wash my hands in a small, dirty sink. It's a little after eight. There are still distinct knocking sounds to be heard, but now I hardly notice them anymore. Occasionally they stop, but I only realize they've been gone when they start again.

When I come out of the restroom, I immediately start researching. I give up starting from scratch, but try to collect the numbers that are close to each other and then cross them out on my paper as I check the content. Some of it is trivial, or facts that I already know: that Emily is the secretary, she's from Mexico, her father's name is Diego and her mother's is Salma, that she grew up in Mapimi but went to school in Torreón, that she's interested in men, preoccupied with her looks and likes talking on the phone. She has previously worked in a Whataburger and briefly in a Hooters, a fast food restaurant where the waitresses wear very low-cut tops. He really has been a thorough man, Ronald. Several of the other references are more fleshed out. The revelations stand side by side with the banal listings of biographical data, and you have to be awake to catch them. I'm not, in fact, I doze off from time to time, my eyes close and I don't know how long it will be before I open them again with a start.

As I look up the references, I realize Ronald really had something on most of them. Even if it was just a summer job at Hooters, he's dug it up. He has cut out interviews and the Department's publications and found less fortunate statements. Everything is carefully listed with thorough source references. It would be impossible to accuse him of dishonesty what with all the examples he has managed to dig up. Alison, for example, has in several cases borrowed ideas from students' assignments and published them in journal articles under her own name: "Serenade for a Fake Prophet. A Post Colonial Reading of Hermann Bölling's Oeuvre" is stolen from an exchange student who never discovered it, and in "Hitler's Real Fate" she borrows the entire argument from a PhD student who never dared to make a case out of it. Sigrun has quoted several relatively unknown works almost verbatim without crediting the author. In an analysis of *Ein Bilderbuch für Gross und Klein: Trau keinem Fuchs auf grüner Heid, und keinem Jud bei seinem Eid*, she borrows several crucial points from the researcher, Judith Kellermann. Ronald has written down the quotes so there is absolutely no doubt. There are numerous similar examples, just as there are dozens of examples of Nazi sympathies. I'm not surprised, it's just a matter of transcribing a random conversation in the hallway, or hacking into a computer, which is apparently what he has done.

Under Alison's bio, there is a reference to a lodge that uses the algiz rune as a distinguishing feature. The one Alison wears on the lapel of her jacket in her profile picture in the hallway of the Department. I bring the box to the table. I have to clear the table of papers and empty boxes to make room and collect all the papers I've been through in a pile next to the table. So much for the systematic approach, painstakingly built up over several decades.

I take the lid off the box, which is the size of a baby bathtub. As far as I can tell, the boxes in the archive come in three different sizes, with this being the largest.

There are several items in the box: pictures, papers, magazines, swastikas, notebooks and a passport stating that Ronald joined the Brotherhood in 1987. There is a picture of him in a white shirt with the algiz rune applied to his stiff collar. There is a hole cut in the passport, so apparently he resigned at some point. The passport is signed Sigrun Walter, chairman, and Alison Fuchs, vice-chairman. Tim and Hermann are also featured in several of the photos.

It goes without saying that he didn't get much published himself. This work must have taken ages, but it was worth the effort. As mentioned earlier, he quickly became a full professor, got a good parking space and the best corner office in the Department—and was left alone. His research could ruin most people's careers. "Academic dishonesty" is the worst insult and the greatest sin in academia.

I'm about to get started on the Lodge's bylaws when my eyes glaze over something again. I just have time to register that "The purpose of the Lodge is to keep secrets" before fatigue overcomes me. The persistent throbbing has moved to a place a little further to my right, but then it too disappears, fades out, and I open my eyes heavily. I must be dreaming, I think.

Deep Blue Velvet

I must be dreaming that they come floating down the hallway. Alison is the first. She's wearing her academic robe, deep blue in shiny velvet, with a pointed hood and an orange cross ribbon. I can't see her whole face, but I can make out her sagging breasts under the robe. She is followed by Jenny, who is also wearing her dress, a frilly pink thing with a train and brown ribbon. They hover a few centimeters above the floor and I can't see their feet, only their festive robes barely touching the floor. The rest of the colleagues from the Department follow, all dressed in gowns of their respective universities, that is, the one from which they received their highest academic degree. Normally, the gowns are only worn for graduation or on special occasions just a few times a year, but now they have apparently seen a golden opportunity to taking them out of the closet. Some wear them more naturally than others, and it's easy to detect a sense of self-esteem by their straight backs and jutting chests, slightly raised chins and lazy eyes. There's no sense of recognition in their eyes. No smiles, no greetings. It's as if I've never met them before. This is strictly business. I recognize Dusty, whose chair I broke the last time I was at her house and who now has to constantly adjust her light purple hood to keep it from falling over her eyes.

They encircle me. Jenny has brought her regalia, which I have never seen before. The Head of the Department's sign of power: a sceptre of sorts and a fine book in leather binding with gold writing. She raises the sceptre and everyone falls silent. Even Alison, standing right next to her, shows reverence for the action and Jenny's ceremonial power. She bites her full lower lip but remains silent.

"Why did you kill Ronald?" Jenny asks. The voice sounds strangely distant, as if it is coming from somewhere else. From where she draws her power, perhaps.

"I'm not sure that I did."

"Ronald wrote you killed him."

"How could he know that?"

"Be careful what you say. Ronald was a professor and an honorable member of our Department."

"I didn't kill Ronald," I say. It won't help to elaborate

on it too much. People will often believe what you say, as long as you say it firmly enough. I frown.

"Memory is subjective," Jenny replies.

"So is reality."

"That's what the people who flew into the Twin Towers on September 11th believed, too. If you think you can bend reality, you'll end up in trouble."

I need to wake up. I wake up and look down the empty hallway. It's still completely silent. I yawn and stretch, but then I see Hermann standing some distance away from me. Along with Jenny and Alison. They look serious, just standing still, as if waiting for me to say something. Jenny is still wearing her cape, the others are wearing their street clothes. I try to say hello, but it comes out wrong. I don't know how much of the dream is real, so I'm not sure how to start. Did we just have a long conversation or have they just arrived? I get the feeling it's not worth asking.

"We have something we want to show you," Jenny says. She nods to Alison, who wheels a TV in front of me. She's already plugged it in and put in a DVD, but she can't get it to work. I'm about to step in to help before it gets embarrassing, but then Hermann takes the remote from her and presses the right button. He does it very discreetly. It's impossible to feel humiliated in his company.

"We've given a copy of this tape to the police," Alison says as Ronald appears on the screen in his office. He's sitting at his desk working on his computer when there's a knock at the door. Ronald gets up, pushes his chair back and stretches. He looks tired. He walks over to the door and opens it, and it's clear he knows the person standing outside. He smiles a slightly forced smile and gestures with his back to the camera. There is no sound in the footage. The next scene shows me walking into the office, my hand is raised and in that very same moment Ronald is slammed to the floor with *Mein Kampf*. The images aren't the best quality, but there is plenty of footage of me sitting next to Ronald's bleeding body, and a little later of me wiping my fingerprints off the places I touched. Then the movie ends abruptly and I look up without saying anything.

"The police will be here in half an hour," Alison says softly. I can see she has to suppress a smile. She must be very pleased with how things are going.

"How could you?" Jenny asks, but Hermann grabs her by the shoulder.

"It's the police's job to find out," he says.

"How could you?" Jenny repeats, and it looks like she's about to cry. She looks genuinely touched. I didn't even know she had feelings. Hermann intervenes again before I can respond.

"You can think about what you've done alone until the police arrive," he says, pulling Jenny towards the door.

Something I Read

As soon as the door is closed behind them, the knocking sounds start again. They are quite close now and I walk over to where they are coming from. It's not so hard to locate the spot anymore because plaster has started to fall from the wall a few meters behind the workbench. I sit down, leaning against the bookcase opposite the wall. I'm so fucking tired I almost don't care that the police will be here in half an hour. I wonder if I'll go straight to jail? I've heard terrible stories about the prison system over here. Two million Americans are behind bars as we speak, and they are not exactly being pampered. Sure, there is a lot of discrimination, like everywhere else in the world, the poor and black people are usually given the longest and toughest sentences, but as a foreigner and a murderer, I probably shouldn't expect to get a TV in my room. This story has taken an unfortunate turn, and while I'm trying to recapitulate exactly where it all went wrong, a blunt tool breaks through the wall. Some debris falls to the floor and everything goes downhill from there. I can hear groans from the other side as larger pieces of mortar and brick falls to the floor in a small pile. Work is now in full swing and the digging tool is hammering through the wall several times with great force, creating a neat hole. Gradually, I can also see part of the digger's arm, then his upper body, then the whole person squeezing through the hole with dust and debris all around him. He's not very tall, quite stocky and completely covered in brick dust. He spits a few times on the floor and wipes some of the dust off his face. Philip, I think.

"Who are you?" I ask hesitantly.

"You're not going to tell me you've forgotten? That I haven't made a bigger impression on you than that?"

"I thought it was something I'd read," I say disillusioned.

"Read and read," Philip says cryptically. "I put a tracker on you before you ran away, and now I could see you were in the sewer network. I had to dig through the last bit. The tunnel had disappeared, the ceiling had collapsed and obliterated the cavity."

I nod. There was something in the notes about Ronald cutting off his son again.

"Maybe I overreacted a little when I tied you up and locked you in. I just wanted to scare you. But then you disappeared. Are you okay?"

"I honestly don't remember much. How did I get out?"

He smiles. "There's no need to probe into that." We look at each other in silence. I had gotten used to the constant knocking, so the silence suddenly feels wrong now.

"The police are on their way," I say dejectedly. "I've lost."

All I want to do is close my eyes and let myself be engulfed by a random dream. Preferably something with Angelina again, her bottom and full lips, and me leaning against a cold basement wall, or me in her bed as Clint Eastwood.

"Do you realize my father is the one who built the archive?" Philip asks, pointing across the room. He looks a little lost, like he's reminiscing. He doesn't react when I answer "Yes," but then gives a little shake, as if to shake off the unreality.

"You were able to guess that?"

"Yes, but I only found out recently. It's an impressive piece of work he's done here."

"I told you he was a smart man. Can you see now what I told you about him is true?" He sits down next to me. He's still wearing his coveralls, but the luminous material has fallen off the M and it's been worn down by the trip through the tunnel.

"We probably had different experiences with him. But I really liked being with him. I can say that without lying, even though he has subsequently managed to get me into a lot of trouble."

"He never told you about me?"

I hesitate. What does one say? "He told me several times he had a son with whom he had reconnected, but I didn't know it was you he was talking about. That I already knew you."

"I was actually the one who went to see him." He didn't say anything about that. But he seemed happy that he had had the "opportunity to get to know you". It's as if the words come naturally. It's all a lie, I think, but Ronald is dead, and I see no reason to tell the truth if I can help the boy move on that way. "I'm glad to hear that," he says. "He was the one who installed me in the motel and showed me the listening equipment. But I didn't really see much of him after that. We chatted occasionally, but there was hardly any physical contact between us in the last few years. He was too busy".

"Busy" might not be the first word I would use to describe Ronald. Cozy, distant, ironic, alcoholic or two-faced, but not busy.

"I didn't see much of him either," I say.

In Capital Letters

Just then, there's a loud knock on the door. "Maybe we can wait with the rest of the story?" I suggest. "Someone has made a date with the police for me."

Philip stands up. "Holy-yodeling Judas," he mutters, "you never have a moment's peace."

"Sorry. But you'd better hurry back out through your passage. These are my problems, and I have to sort them out myself."

"I've come to rescue you. I'm not going to abandon you now that I've arrived in time. Besides, I can prove your innocence," he says casually.

There's a knock on the door, and this time there's also a gruffy-sounding voice that in a cliché-like way shouts: "It's the police. You have exactly ten seconds to open the door or we'll break it down." The man on the other side of the door starts counting backwards from ten. In big letters: "TEN ... NINE ... EIGHT ..."

Philip offers me a hand and pulls me up. Then he pulls me along to the hole, "FIVE ... THREE... I'm warning you, sir, TWO," and through it with difficulty.

He tries to push some rocks in front of it, and I help him, but it doesn't really work, the rocks keep rolling down, and meanwhile we hear the man reaching the end of the countdown: "ONE, please step away from the door," whereupon there is a huge bang as he hammers his shoulder against the door, and it smashes open at the first attempt. He must be a big man. A little later we hear him shouting, "Come out, you have nowhere to run," and then the sound of more voices agreeing with him. Then the sound of a dog barking.

We start crawling through the first part of the passage. It's as narrow as a fox's den, I think, and this time my sister isn't here to pull me out by my legs. Instead, there are a couple of big policemen to do that, I'm sure, which motivates me to get moving, so I crawl on after Philip, and soon the passage widens and we're back in the sewer system where it all started. Behind us, we can hear several dogs that have started howling. They have already found the hole and are on the track of our scent. You can no longer hear what the men are saying, but you can still hear their voices as an echoing murmur reverberating through the passage.

"This is your last warning, kid," says one of the policemen. He is using a megaphone so you can't escape hearing it. "Stop or we'll shoot," the shouter yells after he has removed the megaphone, like a guitar that's too close to the loud speaker at a rock concert. Then the sound of a gunshot going off in the passage can be heard, they mean business.

My heart skips a beat before it starts pounding. "Let's go," Philip says and starts running. I follow. The path slopes downwards and we quickly pick up speed, with long, descending strides downwards until we hit the water where the sewer really begins. And with it the stench of shit. Behind us, the dogs are yelping, and we can hear running footsteps and, far behind, see the flickering glow of a handheld flashlight on the sides of the corridor. "The dogs will have a hard time tracking us in the water," Philip shouts sensibly. The water rises around us as we run through the sewer. This time we're not suffering from cold feet or an indefinable shiver running down our spines. We're filled with nothing but pure terror, the fear of dying and our hearts racing at full speed.

THE DISTANT ECHO

We've been running around the hallways for what feels like ages. We've had to change direction several times because we've heard our pursuers nearby, the howls of dogs and running feet in the water, as well as seen the occasional floodlight over the walls when a pursuer passes an adjacent hallway in the labyrinth. Philip seems very confident. He turns at small passages several times that lead into a sewer pipe that runs parallel to the main line. Once we have to kneel down on all fours to get through, and another time we have to climb a ladder to get to a smaller pipeline. Gradually, we see flickering lights and hear our pursuers. Only echoes of distant dog yelps remain, echoing indefinitely in the corridors.

Philip climbs up another ladder and removes a grate blocking the way into an air duct.

"Here we are."

He's out of breath, but no more than I am, and he seems less affected by the whole situation.

"Great," I say, trying to control my breathing. "I really owe you."

"No, you don't."

Philip puts the grille in place after I've maneuvered my way past him. It snaps into place with a click. I continue on in the duct. It leads to the control room, where we sat together at the computer and flew over Texas a long time ago. The canal ends a few meters above the floor, but there's a ladder hanging on the wall you can climb down. I climb down, and a little later Philip follows. Once he's down, he picks up a white plate from the floor and climbs up and puts it in place in the hole, sealing off the sewer. You can't even see the cracks—or hear the distant echo of the dogs. Except in your mind. It's like it never happened.

Philip turns on the nearest monitors on the table along the wall. He presses a keyboard and images from two surveillance cameras from the sewer appear. Occasionally, a policeman or a dog passes by, but you can tell they are giving up the chase. Even the dogs look perplexed, sniffing the air and they can't seem to remember if they've been there before or if it's their own scent they are picking up.

"Would you like a beer and a slice of cold pizza?" Philip asks.

"There's nothing in this world I'd like better". Philip walks over to the fridge, which he opens with difficulty. As if someone has just opened it and the door is still clinging to the frame with its suction cup lips. He looks at me hesitantly, but then grabs two beers from the top shelf and brings them back. "Pizza's over there," he says, pointing to the table next to the computer. "There's cheese on the crust."

I go over and open the lid of a large pizza box. There's half a pizza with ham, mushrooms and solidified melted cheese. It doesn't look enticing, but I'm hungry, so I take a slice and sit next to Philip, who is in front of the computer screens.

We drink our beers in silence and I eat my pizza. Meanwhile, we watch surveillance footage, but no one passes by anymore. They must have given up.

"They've probably given up," Philip says. He takes the last sip of his beer.

"Should I go get another one?" I ask, but he shakes his head.

"Wouldn't you rather know who killed my father?" he asks. "I have it all on tape."

"I've already seen it," I say. "It shows it was me who did. And if it really was, I don't even know what to say to you. I can't believe I don't remember it, and I'm unable to detect the slightest urge to kill within me."

"You're not the one who did it. I've already told you, I have the evidence that proves your innocence."

"It's interesting because I have an inexplicable feeling of guilt in my body. They've really convinced me I'm the one who did it." Apart from the guilt, the only thing I feel is the urge to cry. But I don't say that.

Philip looks at me for a long time. Then he turns to the computer and types some commands, double-clicks on an icon and says: "Here it is, take a good look. It's probably pretty much the same sequence you've seen, but it was definitely manipulated. Alison used to work at a local TV station where she learned how to cut and edit. And manipulate," he adds with a smile.

"I didn't know that, but I don't know her very well, either."

"She actually taught me how to edit digitally. My dad thought it would be good if I could do the most basic things myself. Like cutting out unnecessary material and stuff like that, so I wouldn't drown in all that information. She spent a few hours teaching me the basics a couple of years ago. My dad convinced her to help, but I don't think it was out of the kindness of her heart."

"I didn't even know she had a heart," I say, and he smiles again.

Then he starts the playback, which opens in a small window on the screen.

RONALD'S DEATH AGAIN

The scene is, of course, the same as in the version I've already seen, once. Ronald is working, someone knocks, he gets up, looks tired, opens the door. But this time it's not me who enters. Ronald smiles and gestures, and Tim enters. They chat for a while before Tim takes *Mein Kampf* out of a bag. He shows it to him, and I can hardly take it, because Ronald nods and is so welcoming, and the next moment Tim raises the book in the air with his arms extended and slams it into Ronald's head.

I can see how this version looks more real than Alison's. There are no cuts and you see it all from the same angle, the whole sequence of Tim killing Ronald, not just my arm. I didn't notice when I watched the other version.

Ronald falls slowly to the floor in an odd sort of way, but he lands with great force as his head slams down hard and he lies lifelessly on the floor. Some blood begins to flow out of his mouth and ear. Tim looks at him coldly. He bends down and examines him before turning around and calling out softly into the hallway.

A moment later, Alison and Sigrun enter. They nod in acknowledgment to Tim before standing around Ronald in a circle of conjuration. Their lips move silently. Then Alison takes *Mein Kampf* out of Tim's hand, who at this point looks a little dejected. She knocks it on Ronald's head and passes it to Sigrun, who does the same. Then Alison takes it back and finally drops it next to Ronald. Then the screen goes black.

I look over at Philip, who has stood and is pacing a little back and forth behind me.

"Half an hour later you come in, but I haven't brought that with me. I don't think there's any reason for that. But you can get a copy so you can get your life back." His voice is mushy and his eyes are a little shiny. I myself can hardly say anything.

"Thank you," I stammer. "I don't know how to thank you. If there's anything I can help you with, please let me know."

"You've already helped me more than you know." He hesitates. It is clear that he is very moved. "But now I think you should go. I'm sure there's someone waiting for you." He hands me a DVD with a copy of Ronald's death.

I nod, not quite knowing why I'm nodding. I go to hug him, but it's too awkward, so I pat him awkwardly on the shoulder. He stands stiff and looks terribly lost in his coveralls. He tries to smile. "Take care of yourself," he says when I'm halfway out of the room. I turn and raise my arm to him. As I turn the corner into the sewer, I can hear him crying.

Angelina Who Is Waiting

Of course, it's Angelina waiting for me when I finally emerge from the sewer. It takes a while to get out, but strangely enough, I can remember part of the way and recognize several things. I have a female memory and recognize the way, instead of remembering the number of meters and when to turn to the right and when to the left like a real man.

Angelina is packing the car when I emerge from the hole. "It wasn't a rental car at all," she says. She's wearing big sunglasses and it looks like she's been crying. I walk up to her but don't say anything. I'll let her break the silence because I honestly don't know what to say.

"Philip is my half-brother," she begins, "if you hadn't already guessed." She looks better than I remembered her. It's as if she's lost weight, and the dark sunglasses and slightly troubled expression suit her.

"Not at all. But there's not much in this story I've been able to guess."

"I understand. It's also turned out pretty grotesque. We were just supposed to pick you up and find out what kind of guy you were, but then things got out of hand.

We were supposed to keep you and film you a bit so Dad could study you. He actually saw you briefly when we stopped at a gas station on the way here. You were asleep."

"I think I actually saw him too. In the rear view mirror."

"But then you fainted in the parking lot and Philip felt he had to improvise. I guess he also saw a connection to Dad through you. Now that Dad had chosen you, he wanted to get to know you better. He's obsessed with Dad and I guess he's also a little off."

"I really like him. It takes a while to get to know him," I add, thinking of the taser gun that sent me to the floor.

"I'm glad you think so. Dad and I have talked several times about what to do with him, but Dad didn't think he was doing any harm here."

Angelina places a suitcase on the minimal back seat.

"I thought you might want a ride," she says. "If you know where you're going. I have to take care of some things for Dad's funeral in the city."

"I'd love to come along."

"What are you going to do?"

"First I need a shower and a good night's sleep in my own bed".

"I think so, too," she interrupts. "You look like hell."

"And then I'm going to the university. They can't touch me if I let them know I have the tape. I think I'll put it on a website with a password I can share with a select few."

"That's good thinking."

"I'm definitely not going back to Denmark right now. I need to have the end of the story with me."

"Of course."

We look at each other for a moment. It's funny that it's like seeing an old friend again, I think. Something happens to friendships when you've had sex. For better or worse, you've crossed an intimate boundary that changes the tone of the conversation. Or maybe it's just the events of the last few days that have created a different resonance.

"Losing my father has knocked me out a bit," she says, "but he told me what was going to happen. He was very clear about it himself and was kind of looking forward to seeing his plot unfold. So in a way, we should be excited, but at the same time, I've lost a father."

I put my arm around her. "I really do understand you. It doesn't change how he felt. Grief is selfish, and it should be."

"But it's so petty not to be happy for him," she says. I give her a hug and she turns towards me and rests her head on my shoulder.

"Well, I won't get a funeral organized standing here like this," Angelina says, and pulls away. She opens the door on my side before walking around and getting into the driver's seat.

"Oh yeah. Dad asked me to give you this," she says, handing me a plastic bag. It's a script, I realize, as she starts the Mustang with a roar and rolls out of the motel.

The electric crackling of the "-otel" sign is flashing.

CONCLUSION

It's amazing what a little harmony will do.
David Crockett

The last part of the manuscript shows who did what and why. Of course, it is important for me to emphasize that much of what follows is unsubstantiated. I guess as a scholar one can't take the content of a novel at face value. However, on the face of it, it is very much in line with my understanding of the events, and I do have some insight into the story.

Ronald knew exactly what was going to happen when there was a knock on the door. As good supporting characters, Tim, Sigrun and Alison simply did what they were meant to do. Not to mention me, who was his most predictable piece in the game. I'm every bit as naive as I'm made out to be. I found him as I was meant to, I found the novel in the drawer, and Hermann found me in the AV room. It's as if my destiny has been controlled from above and my free will has been momentarily suspended...

Ronald's membership in the Lodge was not a success. He was only a member for a year, mainly to obtain material for the archives, which had become an obsession for him. He did manage to have a relationship with Agatha, the name of the woman with the blonde hair, but what came of that is not discussed in the novel and I don't want to think further about the possible consequences of the encounter.

There were enough reasons to murder Ronald. The decision was made at a Lodge meeting a few months ago, after Alison was told by me Ronald was writing a book about the Department. He told me to get the story going. Alison then got Paulina to question Ronald one night when she was supposed to be with him, and Paulina reported to Alison everything she had been told. Unsuspectingly. Alison is an excellent manipulator.

Alison presented the case very dramatically to the members of the lodge and got their support to devise a plan to protect their secrets, "by any means necessary" as they say. She chose to go low-tech. They made a toss up to determine who was going to swing *Mein Kampf* in the air, and Tim won, and that's as far as it goes.

I sleep for a good 24 hours when I finally get home from my surreal excursion. Angelina drops me outside my apartment building and we agree to call each other. We've barely spoken in the car. Angelina is thinking about her dad and I'm exhausted. I rummage around for my keys for a long time and feel like I'm about to pass out several times. When I get into the apartment, I go straight to the bedroom and fall into bed with my clothes on. That must be how it happened, because that's how I find myself the next day, along with a pounding headache.

It takes a few days to recover, during which I keep a low profile in my apartment. I take walks along the river looking at turtles and the long brown legs of students, drink coffee at the small cafes in the neighborhood and watch a lot of videos. Then I call my friends. And Angelina. I do that in Ronald's story, so that's how it must be. I think we also have a relationship, several children and a happy marriage on an abandoned farm in Washington State. I don't know how my wife back home in Denmark will feel about that, but I'm not going to call and ask permission. For now, it's just nice to see Angelina and play that we're in love, and then we'll see where it goes from there.

I introduce Angelina to Gunther and he hates her. I know in my heart this is the end of that friendship. It ends up with a falling out at a gay bar downtown, where I look like the disdained lover as I abruptly get up and walk out to the tune of the Pet Shop Boys' *Suburbia*.

After a week has passed, I go to the Department. I'm surprised I haven't been contacted by them, and when I get there, everything is the same. People talk to me as before, no one mentions Ronald, and even the meetings are the same as before, except I no longer make coffee and Ronald is not there. In his place, we hire a very German woman whose "s"'es are voiced and who has a strong CV. She is one of the leading researchers on the Holocaust. She's installed in Tim's office because, of course, he's taking over Ronald's. There's a little twinge in my side the first time I walk past and see the door sign replaced.

It's not entirely true nothing has changed. I can feel my colleagues treat me with more care. Everyone is nice without being obvious, and I'm unlikely to experience any more annoying complaints. Knowledge is power, and of course I have let Alison and the rest of the gang understand what I know and that in the event of my death, my knowledge will be made public. Alison pretends not to understand what I am referring to, but she too changes her behavior. She obviously respects me for playing the game as well as she does.

The police investigation is also terminated, and the basement room apparently never existed. The dean plays poker with the police commissioner and quickly puts an end to the little case. Something about the commissioner having some peculiar sexual desires and frequenting a brothel in the city's Mexican neighborhood.

Several of the police officers who were in the basement inexplicably disappear, others are just as inexplicably promoted. At the same time, the entrance to the basement is sealed

I'm at Ronald's funeral. He is buried in a quiet ceremony at a church in rural Arizona. It could be in a western, and so could we, as we stand with our heads bowed around the white coffin. Above the church wall, you can see some wooden farms on flat fields, which in turn are fenced off by a mountain range further out on the horizon. Some longhorns are grazing in a field next to the church. You can hear the nearest ones chewing grass from where we are standing.

Several people from the Department have made the trip out here. Jenny Kennedy sent an email around. She wanted to represent the Department at the funeral, she wrote, but everyone was welcome to come along—and to contribute to a funeral bouquet from colleagues. The contribution list was being handled by Emily, who carefully wrote down our amount on a slip of paper, all the while smiling her fake smile.

Philip and Angelina are there too, of course, as are Philip's mother and stepfather, who look rather haggard. Neither of them show any signs of emotion as the coffin is lowered into the hole and the priest throws dirt on top of it. The mother stares fixedly at the coffin and I would give anything to be able to read her mind. The stepfather seems to be in another world. I can hear the occasional sniffle, and Jenny takes a handkerchief out of her pocket and wipes her eyes so as not to be emotionally distant from the others.

A raven flies screeching across the sky. It circles once over the church before heading for the mountains. It's almost too much, but that's how Ronald insists the story ends. With the raven screeching and flying towards the mountains, and us standing by his grave following it. With tears rolling down our cheeks, the fresh prairie air blowing in our faces, and Angelina's behind on our minds. At least, as far as I'm concerned. In his coffin, Ronald nods affirmatively.

Nina Sokol is a poet and translator in the midst of translating novels, short stories, plays and poems by Danish writers. She was a grant poet-in-residence at The Vermont Studio Center in 2011. She has received several grants from the Danish Art's Council to translate plays, including a play written by the fairy tale writer H. C. Andersen which was published by the journal "InTranslation." Her own poems have appeared in American journals, including Miller's Pond and the Hiram Poetry Review and a collection is now available from Spuyten Duyvil, *The Silence Sound Makes*.

KRISTIAN HIMMELSTRUP (himmelstrup.info) has an M.A. from both The University of Washington and The University of Copenhagen and has taught language, cultural studies and creative writing at universities in Denmark and the US. He made his debut in 2004 with the novel *Last Tango of the Dinosaur* and has since published further three novels and a collection of short stories along with several books on literature and cultural studies.